The
LUMINOUS FAIRIES
and MOTHRA

Also Published by the University of Minnesota Press

Godzilla and Godzilla Raids Again
Shigeru Kayama
Translated by Jeffrey Angles

The LUMINOUS FAIRIES and MOTHRA

SHIN'ICHIRŌ NAKAMURA
TAKEHIKO FUKUNAGA
YOSHIE HOTTA

Translated and with an Afterword by Jeffrey Angles

UNIVERSITY OF MINNESOTA PRESS
MINNEAPOLIS
LONDON

This book was the recipient of the 2024–25 William F. Sibley Memorial Subvention Award for Japanese Translation from the University of Chicago Center for East Asian Studies Committee on Japanese Studies.

Published by the University of Minnesota Press
111 Third Avenue South, Suite 290
Minneapolis, MN 55401-2520
http://www.upress.umn.edu

ISBN 978-1-5179-2001-2 (pb)

A Cataloging-in-Publication record for this book is available from the Library of Congress.

Printed in Canada on acid-free paper

34 33 32 31 30 29 28 27 26 10 9 8 7 6 5 4 3 2

Contents

Note on Japanese Names

All Japanese names in and on the cover of this book are presented in the Western order (given name followed by family name) instead of the order usual in Japan (surname followed by given name). For example, the author of the first part of the novella is known in Japan by the name Nakamura Shin'ichirō, but his estate prefers that in this book his name appears in the English order Shin'ichirō Nakamura.

The
LUMINOUS FAIRIES
and MOTHRA

A Lovely Song from a Little Beauty in the Grassland

Shin'ichirō Nakamura

Shin'ichi Chūjō was still lying face-up in his bed on the ship. He took a first puff of his cigarette but immediately set it aside, placing it in the ashtray beside his bed. After feeling around for the large booklet by his pillow, he picked it up and gazed at the cover for a few moments. Every day so far of this monotonous trip he'd done the same thing, but tomorrow this little habit would come to an end. This was the last time he'd reread it. Tomorrow, the research vessel he was on would reach its destination: Infant Island.

Reference Materials for the Japanese-Rosilican Joint Research Expedition

He gazed at these words on the cover for a moment as if to satisfy himself before flipping the pages open. He had read and reread the booklet countless times, and the pages always opened to the same spot. Printed across the top of the page were the words "Brief Accounts of the Four Survivors of the *Gen'yō-maru.*"

Not long ago, the *Gen'yō-maru,* a midsize cargo transport, had been caught in Typhoon No. 8, which sunk it to the bottom of the ocean. A few hours before that happened, a careless mishap on the part of the radio operator had started a fire that left part of the communications room in cinders. It was a disaster. The communications equipment stopped working, and the backup radio equipment and replacement parts were rendered useless. Meanwhile, a storm arose and quickly escalated into a Type-A typhoon, but because of the equipment failure, the *Gen'yō-maru* didn't get the urgent warning telling all ships in the region to evacuate. As a result, the ship lost its chance to escape.

Such things weren't necessarily completely unheard of. It was the bizarre turn of events that took place next that stunned the entire world. Four second officers from the *Gen'yō-maru* washed onto the nearby shores of Infant Island. When a rescue team reached them, expecting to find nothing but corpses, much to their surprise, they found the four crew officers alive and well.

How could they have survived? The rescue party was astounded. When they saw the survivors rush to shore, dressed in tattered clothes and shouting at the top of their lungs, they couldn't believe their eyes. Some members of the rescue mission later recounted that they thought they'd been hallucinating. In recent years, the nation of Rosilica had been testing out its new arsenal of hydrogen bombs on Infant Island. Wind and heat from the repeated bomb blasts had repeatedly ripped across three-quarters of the island, so everyone had assumed it was impossible to survive there for very long.

In the account printed in the booklet, this is how the crew members described their experiences.

When we regained consciousness, we weren't on shore. We were in some sort of odd room. It was rather spacious, and we could see the walls were made of stone. We thought we must be in a hollowed-out space in an underground cave. We'd been laid to rest on something that resembled a bed covered with piles of some unfamiliar plant.

As we came to our senses, we realized there were five or six people nearby. When they saw us get up, they let out a strange cry that's nearly impossible to describe. They were people—not all that different from us—but, to put it succinctly, they looked like the kind of indigenous people you might find in the undeveloped world. We couldn't communicate with them at all. They had prepared a thick, boiled soup, which they made us drink. We all had several bowls. It didn't taste especially bad, and we didn't really think we were in danger. To be honest, we were all so hungry that we asked for refills. We couldn't help ourselves. Next, they made us eat the fruit of some kind of plant—quite a lot of it too.

They tried to communicate with us using body language and gestures. They seemed to be telling us, "This island is dangerous, but you're safe now." After we were rescued, we learned some things that really surprised us. We think the danger they were talking about probably had to do with radiation sickness. However, when we got back to Japan, we were checked out at the National General Research Center, and they told us we weren't showing any signs of radiation sickness. In fact, we had more strength than usual. We can't help but think that the soup and fruit we were given had some special, medicinal effect.

The only natives we saw were those five or six people with us, but it's safe to assume there were more. They started leading us up a staircase. There were so many stairs that we realized the room must've been deep underground. There's something that still strikes us as strange. There were no electric lights, kerosene lamps, or other devices to light the place up, so why was the underground room so bright? When we emerged into the sunlight again, the natives had completely disappeared. That's when we saw the rescue team. We were saved!

There was a knock on the door, and Professor Harada, a specialist in nuclear science, stepped into Chūjō's room. "Say there, you look nice and relaxed." A smile crept over his ruddy cheeks.

"I'm jealous of you guys. You get together in the canteen every day to talk about all sorts of things." Chūjō got up from where he lay.

The joint expedition to Infant Island had been arranged by the Japanese and Rosilican governments, so there were physicists, biologists, doctors, and anthropologists from both countries on board. Chūjō, however, was the only linguist. The plan was to have him study the language of the indigenous inhabitants. Even a little understanding would no doubt help the expedition's work go a lot faster, but the fact that Chūjō was the only linguist aboard meant that there wasn't a lot of need for him to spend time with the specialists in other disciplines.

Harada furrowed his brow. "That guy Nelson seemed really unhappy during the meeting earlier."

"What the heck is his area of expertise anyway?" Chūjō asked.

Nelson was one of the participants in the expedition. Apparently his role was to handle arrangements and necessary details for the Rosilican participants. He spoke Japanese well, but he had a haughty attitude, which sometimes left the Japanese members of the expedition with a bad taste in their mouths.

"Maybe he belongs to some secret organization. . . . Our goal, however, is to go there for purely scientific purposes." Harada put his hands down on the back of a backward-facing chair, straddled the seat, and added, "Having a guy like him on board makes me suspicious about whether the Rosilican government is really acting in good faith."

Chūjō whispered, "Japan isn't a Rosilican colony." As he recalled the cruel glint in Nelson's eyes, he added, "That guy's got the eyes of a killer," and with that, his voice trailed off.

The next morning, a gong reverberated across deck. All at once, everyone started preparations to land.

Their bodies were encased in a new type of protective gear designed to protect them from radiation. The suits were equipped with a tiny siren. Just push the button and it would make a loud sound, alerting everyone to danger. The bright, clear alarm ought to be audible over quite a distance.

With worried expressions on their faces, the expedition members silently boarded the landing craft. Dr. Raff, the physicist who was serving as expedition leader, glared at the island and muttered to himself, "This island. . . . It really lets you feel its hidden anger. It also seems to be pleading somehow, like it's lonely or something."

Chūjō's task was to do his best to locate the native population and to examine the patterns of their language. The stories of the survivors from the downed boat were clear: they had encountered an indigenous group on the island. Before the hydrogen-bomb tests, the generally accepted consensus had been that Infant Island was uninhabited. As a result, the Rosilican government conducted its hydrogen-bomb blasts without raising much alarm; however, it was now obvious that this information had been wrong. If the four survivors from the *Gen'yō-maru* weren't crazy, there must be an indigenous population hidden on the island somewhere.

The scientists went ashore at the landing site and immediately got to work. Chūjō, however, went on ahead, venturing into the grassy interior on his own. He didn't know the name of the type of extra-tall grass that surrounded him, but it stretched high above his head. It was hard to believe that a grassy field could grow so tall like this so soon after the hydrogen-bomb tests.

An ominous feeling suddenly came over him. A snake? No, that wasn't it. Right in front of him were a bunch of vines covered in bright, garish flowers. The vines spread out and flexed like the legs of a cephalopod or some such creature. The tendrils were feeling out their environment like a blind man using a cane to navigate his surroundings. Little by little, the vines stretched toward him.

Chūjō jumped into the air.

In that same instant, a vine that had raised its head for the attack wrapped around him. It all happened in the blink of an eye.

Chūjō grabbed the vine, wanting to tear it off, but another one quickly snaked around his arm, as if it knew exactly where to aim. On the tips of the vines he could see mouths that looked like suction cups. They writhed around, exuding some sort of mucus.

A vampire plant! The suckers were trying to drink his blood. Right away, a group of vines began slowly wrapping themselves around Chūjō's body. Using what little remained of his freedom, he managed to move his fingers far enough to press the button on his chest.

By the time the other members of the expedition came rushing to his aid, the vines had completely encircled Chūjō, who was gazing up at the flowers in a sort of daze. The upper part of his body was swaying as if he were intoxicated—the work of the vines, no doubt.

"Chūjō!" Harada exclaimed. "What happened?"

Chūjō tried to explain that he had been struggling against the bloodsucking plant this whole time, but he was so exhausted and weak that his story came out in fits and starts. "But if those small, strange people hadn't appeared, I would've been a goner."

The expedition leader shot back, "Who are you talking about? You don't mean the natives, do you?"

"No, judging from the reports of the survivors, the natives are probably around the same size as us. These people were much shorter—they were someone else . . ."

A biologist asked, "Are you sure they weren't just kids?"

"No, they looked like adults. Tiny women, unimaginably small. Only about fifty or sixty centimeters . . ."

"What?" Nelson shouted. "Dwarf women?" Like a hunter, he narrowed his eyes and looked about with a frenzied gaze as a disturbing smile rose to his lips.

• • •

That night, when everyone was back on the ship, the group engaged in a heated debate about how to organize and record the results of their initial survey.

Chūjō had returned to the boat, still wearing the same dazed expression he had when he stood there all alone, transfixed in front of those garishly colored flowers. He stood on deck by himself, away from the other expedition members, looking down into the ocean.

Two fellow passengers were walking by with hurried footsteps, but they stopped behind Chūjō and asked, "What's the matter?" One of them was Harada, the nuclear scientist.

Still silent, Chūjō lifted his head but didn't turn around.

"You don't seem well at all." Worriedly, Harada asked, "Don't you think you should go see the doctors and have them look you over?"

In a brisk voice, the other colleague turned to Harada and said, "Say, that thing we were just talking about. . . . Let's investigate further when we go ashore again tomorrow." Then he disappeared down the stairs.

Chūjō gave a distracted, preoccupied smile and said, "I'm not sick. It's just that what I saw today was so unlike anything I've ever imagined." He spoke as if he were talking half to himself.

"It's possible those flowers had some sort of narcotic properties. You seem drunk or intoxicated somehow." As he spoke, Harada lit a cigarette.

"No, I don't have a headache. I'm not unsteady on my feet or anything." Chūjō spread his legs slightly, planted his feet on deck, and stood up straight to make his case.

"But you experienced some kind of visual hallucination under the influence of those flowers . . ."

"No, I wasn't hallucinating. I'm positive—I saw two little women. You'll see tomorrow."

"What're you going to do? You're going back to that grassy field again? If you do, I'll go too."

"Please do, I'll show you I wasn't just seeing things."

Harada furrowed his brow and put his hand on Chūjō's shoulder. "In any case, you should get a good night's rest tonight."

Chūjō opened his eyes wide and said, "I'm looking forward to tomorrow." This time, he spoke with confidence in his voice.

The sky was bright overhead as a siren went off, echoing across the landscape. Thinking that another colleague must have been caught by the bloodsucking plants, the scientists on the seashore rushed toward the noise.

Chūjō and Harada were in front of the flowers from yesterday. This time, Harada was the one standing still as a statue. Chūjō called out to all the scientists running in his direction. "Look! Proof of the little women!"

Everyone looked where he pointed. Standing on the ground was a tiny little woman, just over sixty centimeters tall, looking up at them all. Her chest and hips were those of a beautiful lady, but as she looked around at the gathered crew members, her tiny eyes seemed to flash with a mysterious brightness.

"My experiences yesterday led me to guess that these beautiful little women are extremely responsive to sound, so I tried sounding my siren. The experiment worked! She showed up just like before. And here she is! No reason to doubt me anymore."

Everyone looked down with amazement at her—a marvel of nature.

Suddenly, the *shōbijin*—the beautiful little lady—began to speak.[1] Well, perhaps "speak" isn't the right word. What she did was closer to singing. A clear, musical voice began to flow from her tiny mouth—a voice completely unlike any that had ever emerged

---

1. The neologism *shōbijin,* used here and in fandom to refer to the Infant Island fairies, is a combination of the kanji meaning "little" (*shō*) and "beauty" or "beautiful lady" (*bijin*).

from human vocal cords before—and as she sang, her arms and legs began to move as if dancing in time to her words.

Chūjō observed her body language while listening attentively to the melody. Without shifting his gaze away, he commented, "Her language doesn't fit into any language family. It's completely its own thing. It just has a subject and predicate. It's less like a language than some sort of code. . . . It seems like she's trying to ask us whether or not there will be any more hydrogen-bomb tests."

She stopped singing, looked up at Chūjō, and gave a smile. Her expression, so full of trust, filled his heart with indescribable happiness. Without even thinking, he extended his hand toward her.

Right then he heard someone speak up behind him. With obvious irritation, Raff the expedition leader said, "Chūjō, tell her that the island no longer has any value as a testing ground."

Chūjō just silently shook his head, sorry that he didn't know how to translate the message into a melody like hers.

A happy expression rose to her tiny face. Chūjō nodded at her over and over, overjoyed that they had been able to communicate after all.

She raised one hand, then tried to dash away.

Right then Nelson jumped in front of her. With his strong, muscular arm, he scooped her up.

"What are you doing?!" Chūjō clamped his hand down on Nelson's shoulder in surprise. "Don't be so rough!"

Nelson turned and gave him a scornful look. "We're here to collect materials and data. She's a valuable find!"

She wriggled around in Nelson's arms and looked up at his face. She seemed to have guessed he might try to grab her. Suddenly she raised a sharp cry, which once again took the form of a magnificent song. Her voice evoked a strange sensation in everyone, making them feel as if they were going to be absorbed into the hot sky above.

Right then someone shouted, “Natives!” A group of dark-skinned, half-naked men and women began to emerge from the tall grass one by one. They wore bloodthirsty expressions on their faces.

Raff, the expedition leader, shouted, “Nelson! Let her go! You’re putting us in danger!”

Nelson made an exasperated sound, but he set the tiny woman back on the ground. Immediately the natives gathered around the *shōbijin*, and an instant later they disappeared back into the grass.

Nelson glared back and forth at Raff and Chūjō. “Why were you so frightened? We’ve got pistols and rifles . . .” His eyes were burning with ugly fervor.

“Nelson!” Chūjō shouted. “There’s no need for violence! You’re not on safari shooting wild animals in Africa. Those are human beings, same as you and me!”

“Human beings?” Nelson held up his hands and sneered at them. “You think those tiny little creatures are human? If that little female is human, I’d like to see you marry her!” A derisive smile rose to his face. “Just think . . . a Jap and a lady dwarf!”

In a sharp voice, Raff shut him down. “Cut it out! You’re acting stupid. I don’t mind debating things scientifically, but I won’t put up with that kind of nonsense.”

The expedition team continued its investigation. Chūjō stayed in the grassy field alone, staring at the tall grass into which the tiny woman and the locals had disappeared. He brought his hand to his chest over and over, thinking he might turn on the siren, but each time, he stopped short. If he sounded it, she’d probably come back. She’d probably look at him again with her special gaze, which evoked so much strange happiness inside him. . . . However, the siren would bring his companions running again, and this time, Nelson might really nab her. Maybe this time, Nelson’s argument that she was just material to be collected—"a valuable find," in his words—might convince the rest of the crew.

Chūjō's thoughts began to drift. He suspected he'd see her again somewhere before the investigation was over. If he could just learn her language, then perhaps he could reach out to her somehow and touch her heart. He thought about how small and sweet the blood-pumping organ inside her tiny body must be. It was too small to be caught up in the filth and corruption of civilization. She was living in a way that had been lost to him and everyone else who deemed themselves "civilized." Her emotions were so pure that she emitted a quiet light. Something in her shone like a pearl.

Suddenly his daydreaming was cut short. He heard a strange melody rising somewhere on the island as if responding to him. It was *that* melody, *her* melody. Yes, it was responding to his thought patterns. No doubt about it. And it kept on going, as if conversing with his thoughts directly.

He rose up and took two or three steps. The singing voice broke off.

Chūjō shouted, "You, the beautiful, little lady . . ."

The song responded to him.

"*Shōbijin!*"

Once again, he heard the same, small melody in response.

"*Shōbijin!* Beautiful, little lady! *Shōbijin!*"

This time, in response to his call, the melody rose from both the east and west sides of the island. Before long, he heard other voices join in from the south and the north, too, adding beautiful harmony to the original melody, forming a single, glorious chorus.

Four Small Fairies on Display

Takehiko Fukunaga

Coast Guard Rescue Ship No. 4, the ship that had carried the research team to Infant Island, pulled back into Tokyo Bay early in the morning only to find a crowd of radio, television, and newspaper reporters already waiting for them. The news outlets had mobilized their representatives and sent them to the piers to greet the scientists.

Ever since Japan and Rosilica sent their most capable scientists to Infant Island, everyone had worried about them developing radiation sickness. After all, lots of hydrogen-bomb tests had taken place there. However, as the scientists filed one by one down the stairs with an energetic spring in their step, the onlookers gave a relieved smile. This seemed promising. The expedition to the lonesome South Pacific island must have yielded successful results.

A large group of reporters pushed forward, desperate to get even the slightest hint of what the expedition had learned, but a stern police presence held them back. First, the expedition team needed to go to the Central Hospital for a careful checkup to see if they were exhibiting any signs of radiation exposure. The only announcement was a short one saying that everyone would have to wait.

The fact that the eager crowd was rebuffed so unceremoniously on the pier of Tokyo Bay, leaving the press without any official statement at all, ended up producing a strange effect. The Japanese press took the situation to mean that the expedition had no doubt made some unexpected, extraordinary discovery on Infant Island. Since the team wasn't authorized to share their findings at their own discretion, the press surmised that the team must be in communication with the Rosilican government. Meanwhile, the newspaper correspondents dispatched from Rosilica to Japan telegraphed back to their home country, sending articles taking the expedition team to task.

Not even a single reporter had been on board when the joint Japanese–Rosilican expedition set out. The *Rosilican Press* pointed this out, arguing that the entire mission had been cloaked in secrecy from the very beginning. As a result, suspicion had been smoldering from the start, but when the expedition came back without a single prepared official statement, people started guessing that something strange was afoot. At least, that was what reporters claimed. The reports from both countries merely heightened the entire world's anticipation. No doubt about that. Before the day was out, people all over the world were burning with impatience.

The following day, Nelson, who claimed information control as one of his responsibilities, held a press conference along with Raff, the expedition leader. Not a single Japanese expedition member was invited. To make matters worse, what Nelson said was very basic, disappointing all the reporters who had been waiting with such impatience. Nelson pointed out that it would take months to compile and summarize all the different types of research the team had conducted. An official report would be forthcoming in three months' time. Until then, the only answer Nelson would give was "no comment." Meanwhile, he gave a strict warning to the reporters not to try to get a scoop by approaching individual members of the expedition.

A reporter from the *Rosilican Press* was the first to protest, but before long, all the reporters stood up, completely enraged.

Nelson didn't have much choice but to give in and permit at least a few simple questions and answers.

"Is it safe to assume that you got the results you expected?"

"Yes."

"Did you detect the effects of the hydrogen bomb on Infant Island?"

"Yes."

"But there was an indigenous population there?"

"Yes."

"Were you able to figure out why?"

"No comment."

"Is there some reason you're being so secretive?"

Nelson didn't say a thing and only shrugged his shoulders.

"Were there any other important discoveries?"

After a moment of hesitation, Nelson responded, "Yes."

With this, he halted all further questions, even though he hadn't yet shared any meaningful information. However, his stern attitude made it clear he was hiding something. Nelson seemed to be clenching his teeth hard, as if biting down. At the end of the press conference, he left the reporters with a single, cryptic utterance: "Don't worry. You'll see soon enough."

Zen'ichirō Fukuda, a society reporter from the *Japan Eastern News*, was one of the many people at the press conference who left profoundly unsatisfied. The Rosilican scientists who had participated in the expedition were immediately called back to Rosilica, so Fukuda chased the Japanese expedition members, following them from their research labs back to their homes. However, none of them granted him easy access. Even if Fukuda did manage to get a word in with them, they stayed tight-lipped and didn't divulge anything fruitful.

Harada, the nuclear scientist, was the only person who gave him any helpful advice, and that was only after Fukuda wore him down with his impassioned entreaties. Half-joking, Harada had said, "You ought to sneak onto Infant Island yourself. Then you'll see!" But then, Harada added, "If you do, you should have Shin'ichi Chūjō teach you the local language. Just remember, if you go, you'll be risking your life!"

Fukuda was a hot-blooded man and took this joke quite seriously.

Chūjō stayed cooped up in his university office, making no effort whatsoever to meet with reporters. Since returning to Japan he had become terribly unsocial, and everyone assumed he was just absorbed in his research. Fukuda, however, succeeded in getting an interview with him by telling Chūjō he had some questions about the distribution of languages in Oceania. In reality, Fukuda didn't know the first thing about linguistics.

A linguist and a reporter. . . . It just so happened that they got along famously, and over the course of a handful of meetings, they developed a warm friendship. That was when Fukuda came clean about his real intentions, telling Chūjō that he wanted to go to Infant Island to conduct his own investigation. He wanted Chūjō to teach him as much as he knew of the local language. Since getting back, Chūjō had been making significant progress by transferring the words he'd captured on his tape recorder onto index cards and classifying them.

"I'm envious," said the young linguist as he stared off into the distance. "I want to go back too."

"Why don't we go together? I'd feel a lot more secure if you were there too."

"We can't. You know, that island's full of radiation. Who knows what might happen?"

"Huh? But if you get in good with the indigenous population, they could give you some of that thick soup, and we'd be fine, right?" Fukuda's expression was as cool as a cucumber.

"There's so much more I'd tell you, if you weren't a newspaper reporter."

"Don't worry. I'm the kind of guy who can keep a promise. Just tell me this. Why's everyone being so secretive?"

"I can't really say."

"Let me guess." An ironic expression came over Fukuda's face. "The Rosilican government has sworn you to silence. They've placed a gag order on all the scientists in the team. You're all university professors—public employees, in other words—so you could face government reprisal if you let something leak. But what I don't get is why the Rosilican government would put so much pressure on you. So . . . what do you say to that?"

Chūjō just looked at him with a noncommittal expression. He made no move to answer.

Fukuda took two months of leave from work before setting off for Infant Island. The question of how he managed to secure transport is outside the scope of this story, but arrangements were made for a ship to come bring him home in thirty days' time.

Before going ashore, Fukuda put on a hazmat suit, covering himself head to toe to protect himself from radiation. Using a map that Chūjō had drawn for him, he headed into the interior of the island. Once it became clear how determined Fukuda was, Chūjō had offered his assistance—at least to a certain extent. He taught Fukuda what he knew of the indigenous language, described the topology of the island, and gave him a stern warning about the dangerous bloodsucking plants. "That's all I can tell you," he said. "You'll just have to see the rest for yourself."

Fukuda was young and fearless. He slowly pushed his way through the tall grass, keeping a careful eye out for bloodsucking plants or anything else that might be dangerous.

Chūjō had been right. The grass was taller than him. As Fukuda crept through, a human form appeared—one that looked back at him with disbelief. However, the discovery of the local population brought Fukuda more relief than surprise.

He tried to start a conversation by repeating the words that he had practiced with Chūjō. They worked. A handful of people who appeared to be natives of the island emerged from the grass and gestured to indicate the way. So far, the adventure was going as planned.

As they emerged from the grassy field, a stretch of mountainous terrain sprawled out before them. Next to a bunch of large boulders was a cave, and Fukuda's guides led him inside. Fukuda had read the accounts of the survivors of the *Gen'yō-maru* so carefully that he had practically memorized them, so none of what he saw next—not the path into the cave, nor the room that seemed to have been hewn from the rock walls, nor the faint phosphorescent glow inside—was completely unexpected. He also wasn't surprised when the locals removed his hazmat suit and gave him some thick soup to drink.

Fukuda was now a guest in their underground cave. He was incredibly grateful to find that, thanks to Chūjō's linguistic research, he could converse with them somewhat. The communication wasn't by any means perfect, but through effort, each side was able to convey the gist of what they wanted to say. The locals seemed to trust Fukuda, and Fukuda, in turn, learned some new things.

It seemed that the local, native population lived with a certain surreal notion of time that didn't make a clear distinction between mythology and reality. When he was a student, Fukuda had been particularly fascinated by comparative mythology and anthropology. In the eyes of uncivilized peoples like these, the world belonged to them, and to them alone. They kept to themselves so thoroughly that the whole world had thought Infant Island was uninhabited, at least until Rosilica started its hydrogen-bomb tests. Apparently, at some point in the distant past, the people of Infant Island had lost contact with the other Pacific islands and had been living there isolated ever since. The myths they shared with Fukuda were quite unusual, so as he listened, he tried to take down as much as possible. At the root of the island's mythology was the following story.

Long ago, when the world was still chaotic and undefined, the first being to appear was the god Ajima, who ruled over the eternal night. He took the things that muddy the world and flow along—things like mist and clouds—and pushed the ones with heavy moisture downward while lifting the light ones high above. In that way, the sea and the sky were formed.

Ajima then lifted something heavy from the bottom of the sea—the ground, in other words—to create two islands. Exhausted from all this work, Ajima lay down on the island that was still nothing but sand, and before long, he was fast asleep and snoring. From his snoring, thunder, violent winds, and tsunamis were born.

On the islands he ruled, eternal night prevailed. He had created the sky, sea, and islands, but he quickly found himself bored, so he split his own body down the middle. The right half of his body was reborn in the same form as before, becoming the same god Ajima who he had always been. The left half, however, was reborn as the goddess Ajigo.

The goddess Ajigo ruled over daytime. She created the sun. As she breathed over the land, the grass, trees, birds, and beasts were born. When she breathed over the sea, fish and other creatures of the sea were born. Feeling a sense of rivalry, the god Ajima created the moon and the stars. However, eventually the two gods found themselves worn out from all the work of creation, so eventually, they lay down together to sleep.

Before long, a gigantic egg was born from their intimacy. Unlike the things which the god and goddess had each created on their own, this egg was born from them both, so it shared characteristics of both day and night. It shone like the sun, and it glowed like the moon. This egg was called Mothra, but it did not hatch, no matter how long they waited.

Next, a male and female couple were born from Ajima and Ajigo. Using their own abilities, the humans gradually began to increase their number until the entire island was overflowing with humanity.

Next, a gigantic number of extremely tiny eggs were born from the god and goddess. These eggs glittered like the stars. The eggs turned into larvae, into chrysalises, and into moths, which flitted about in the air.

The male god Ajima became convinced that it had been a mistake on the part of the female goddess Ajigo to give birth to so many tiny eggs, so he flew into a rage. He cast death down on the world. He cast it down upon everything—upon humanity, the birds, the beasts, and the fish—killing half of everything. Ajima was still so furious that he broke his body into four pieces. The island rumbled, and parts of it collapsed. The four parts of his body flew into the sky, joining the dawn stars, the night stars, the northern stars, and the southern stars in the heavens.

The goddess Ajigo was despondent. As she lamented, she decided to offer her own body as a living sacrifice to Mothra, the Egg of the Infinite, so she came before it and split her body into four parts, and with that, she died. However, from those four parts, four tiny young girls were born, each less than half the height of an ordinary human being. Their entire bodies glowed, even in the middle of the night. These tiny creatures were called Airena, and as maidens in the service of Mothra, the Egg of the Infinite, they had eternal life. When the larvae that had hatched previously from the countless small eggs formed their own cocoons, they took the thread from the cocoons and wove it into clothing for themselves. The threads in those clothes also glowed like phosphorus in the night.

Before she died, the goddess Ajigo uttered a prophecy: "The Airena will serve Mothra, and Mothra will be sure to protect this island."

When Fukuda heard this story from the island elders, his first impulse was to dismiss it as little more than a tale that had nothing to do with reality. Such stories, he thought, were nothing more than cultural relics that had been handed down over the generations from the island's ancestors. Every ethnicity had its own such stories.

One day, however, as he was trying to leave the cave, he took a different path than usual. Somewhere, off in the distance, he detected singing. The music drew him in, and out of curiosity he switched directions and headed deeper into the caves. There was no artificial lighting in the caves, but even so, the path he followed seemed to exude a pale glow. As he walked along, he began to suspect for the first time that the glow might have something to do with the countless glowing tiny eggs, larvae, chrysalises, and moths that had been such an important part of the myth.

As he passed through the last, low part of the tunnel, he experienced a shock so great that words escaped him. He found himself in a deep hollow in the rock surrounded by mountain walls, but the stones in front of him formed what looked like a natural staircase. On the very top step, a gigantic, pale egg was lying on its side, glowing and glittering. Something that looked like a shrine had been constructed below it, and there, four unbelievably tiny women were sitting at looms, weaving cloth. Their bodies, their clothing, and even the cloth they were weaving were all emitting light.

Was this what Chūjō had meant when he'd said Fukuda would just have to see things for himself? The sight was so mysterious and lovely that Fukuda couldn't believe his own eyes. The four tiny women sang in chorus with such beauty that their voices could only be described as angelic.

The next morning, when Fukuda woke, he felt full of joy. However, that didn't last. The natives were running, panicked and shouting, "Airena go away! Airena must not go away!"

Fukuda didn't understand what was happening, but he anxiously ran outside with the natives. A siren was wailing, reverberating across the beach in a single, unbroken tone. It might have sounded pleasant if everyone wasn't so upset.

"Airena must not go away!"

As Fukuda looked across the beach, he saw something terrible. A group of men covered in hazmat suits were pointing pistols and rifles at the natives, who were utterly defenseless with no weapons at all. One of the *shōbijin* he had seen last night had been captured and put in a cage. She was calling out in her sing-song voice. The natives were trying to help her, but the invaders kept shooting them, killing them one by one. It was a massacre, and the locals had no way to resist.

Fukuda heard someone speak. It appeared to be the leader of the invading army.

"That's enough. Let the rest of them run. We'll chase them down eventually. There might still be more little women hidden away somewhere."

Fukuda recognized him. It was Nelson.

In that instant, Fukuda understood what everything meant. Perhaps it was his natural instincts as a reporter, but he could see right through Nelson's nefarious plot. Like the natives, he started to run, but he soon tripped in the thick grass and lost consciousness.

SECRET OF INFANT ISLAND REVEALED

Four Tiny Beauties—Fairies or Angels?

Nelson Holds Press Conference

In no time at all sensational headlines like these appeared on the front pages of all the newspapers in Japan and Rosilica. After a three-month silence, Nelson had gathered reporters from all the news outlets, starting with the *Rosilican Press,* to finally hold a press conference on the materials that the scientists had collected on Infant Island.

"When I talk about the 'materials' we brought back," he said, "what I'm really referring to are the four little fairies I'm about to show you. I don't dare call them 'women.' The only language that they have is song. They're smaller than ordinary human children, but these little creatures are definitely not children. We didn't find any other creatures on Infant Island that appear to be of the same species. These four don't appear to procreate at all. In fact, they seem immortal . . ."

Nelson prattled on for a few more moments before he brought out the four little *shōbijin* beauties—the four "fairies," he called them—and showed them to the press, which by that point was exploding with curiosity. Nelson put them on display for only five minutes, just long enough to let the photographers snap some photos, before whisking them away again. However, the tiny women left an overwhelming impression on everyone.

"I've got something else that might surprise you even more. However, I imagine you'll all see it before long." There was a haughty tone in Nelson's voice as he made this final prediction.

Here is what he meant. Presenting the *shōbijin* to the public would be the best way to prove their existence to the world, so he had planned a show. Although Nelson emphasized its scientific importance, the *Rosilican Press* cynically nicknamed it "The Four Fairy Show." The fairies would be featured in Tokyo's largest theater, and the public could come see them for the price of admission—an amount that turned out to be astronomically high.

The opening day performance, which was supposedly to raise money for charity, was attended by large crowds of people, including the prime minister, the Rosilican ambassador, and lots of aristocratic ladies who had nothing whatsoever to do with the scientific community. When the chimes rang to mark the start of the show, two announcers from Rosilica and Japan gave long speeches. Finally, the lights went out, and the four luminous fairies were brought onto stage. Needless to say, the crowd was amazed.

Some people were outraged by the performance and objected to it on humanitarian grounds. Chūjō was among their number. After returning to Japan, he had found himself losing focus and falling deep into abstracted thought more and more often. This tendency was, of course, related to his encounter with the little ladies on the island. It wasn't that he was in love—no, that wasn't it. He couldn't escape the feeling that he could still hear their voices—their lovely, sing-song voices—somewhere deep inside him. He had hoped that when Fukuda returned, he would bring more information that would help him better understand these emotions.

Even before Fukuda got back, however, certain things had become clear. The Japanese government had prohibited the publication of any research by the Infant Island expedition team. The government of Rosilica was clearly behind this ban, but the Rosilican head of state had not been acting on his own. Nelson hid behind his position as information officer, but considering his rare gift for showmanship, it wasn't hard to figure out that he was the driving force behind the show. How clever he had been in his pronouncements! Even though he already possessed unlimited wealth, this was a big gamble for him—in fact, the biggest gamble he could make. He was betting that the world wouldn't label him an unethical, inhuman monster.

Chūjō made up his mind. He sent word that he wanted to see Nelson. Since Chūjō was a member of the original expedition team, Nelson consented to give him five minutes of his valuable time, but when Chūjō started to lecture him, Nelson's first response was an arrogant, contemptuous smile.

"You think the show is inhumane? . . . Well, those little creatures aren't human! They're *things!* I collected them as part of our research on Infant Island. In other words, they belong to me. You want me to return them to the island? No way! But before you pass judgment, Chūjō, don't you want to at least see the show? Let me give you some tickets. I'll arrange for you to sit in the reserved seats in front so you can take in the performance. You'll see we haven't restrained the fairies in any way whatsoever. They've never expressed a desire to go back. When you see them sing, you'll see that they're as happy as clams."

Chūjō couldn't come up with a counterargument. He felt like his heart was breaking as he stood up. Overcome by the desire to see the *shōbijin* again, he took the ticket and went into the theater. As the lights dimmed, the four fairies began singing in unison. Of all the people gathered in the audience, Chūjō was the only one who could understand the meaning of their chorus, which to everyone else merely sounded like humming. Perhaps he had formed some kind of telepathic communication with the fairy he had met back on the island.

No doubt about it. The fairies' song sounded bright, transparent, and happy on the surface, but there was something else there too. Their song contained a sense of hopeful anticipation, something that seemed like a plea to a supernatural force. Yes, there was a hint of a future that was sure to come, something that would send a chill up everyone's spine.

As if waking from a dream, Fukuda opened his eyes and looked around, but what he saw in the underground cavern looked like it was out of a nightmare. He had been plunged from the heights of his previous happiness into the depths of tragedy. The natives had been massacred. Those who had survived were busy tending to the wounded. The four Airena had been captured and carted away. Fukuda had also been wounded, but the locals had nursed him back to consciousness. Now that he was awake, he experienced bitter heartbreak right alongside them.

The natives no longer tried to hide anything from him. They

led him through a passage to the back of the cave system and the shrine he had discovered. There lay Mothra, the Egg of the Infinite, which shone like the sun during the day and glowed like the moon during the night. There, the natives poured their curses, lamentations, and deepest desires into song as they began to perform some mysterious dance—a ritual that they repeated night after night.

Fukuda felt as if he were still caught in a nightmare, unable to wake up completely. As the days went by, he joined the ritual each night and observed. With each day, the enormous egg seemed to grow even larger, and its light glowed a little brighter.

One night, a tremendous rumbling reverberated throughout the cave. The natives threw themselves facedown, prostrate on the ground, when suddenly a crack appeared in the shell of the egg. An incredibly huge larva emerged. It was cylindrical in shape, with a head stacked on top of its chest and its abdomen. Sure enough, its entire body exuded a pale glow.

"Ajima, the God of the Universe, has been reborn!" The natives raised their voices as if casting a spell. "Mothra, the Egg of Eternity, has hatched! Mothra will surely protect the Airena!"

Meanwhile, the newborn larva began crawling on its eight pairs of legs toward the sea. It moved with such amazing speed that it quickly disappeared from sight. Fukuda stared off into the distance, trying to catch a glimpse of something more, but the only sights that greeted his eyes were the dark shadows of the natives bustling around him, surrounded by the endless darkness of night.

Mothra Reaches Tokyo Bay

Yoshie Hotta

The darkness of night had settled over the ocean. Bathed in moonlight, a single ship was sailing steadily southward. It was clearly a fishing vessel, but from its mast hung the flag of the *Japan Eastern News.* Fukuda's employer had chartered it to go pick him up.

One of the crew members stood on deck, smoking a cigarette under the light of the moon. The ocean waves rose and fell quietly, indicating smooth sailing. There was relatively little sound at sea, so when the sailor heard large waves crashing in the distance, he was immediately alarmed. As he stood tall and pricked up his ears, he caught sight of something that made him question his own eyes. At first, he thought he was seeing a rare white whale—the kind of creature he had only heard about in stories—but no, that couldn't be right. When he grabbed some binoculars for a better view, he found himself even more perplexed. It was whitish, thick, and rounded—definitely not a fish or a whale. Whatever it was, it was enormous, probably around a hundred meters long, and it was swimming through the ocean waters, stirring up waves as it went. It was headed northwest, in the opposite direction.

The sailor ran to the bridge and shouted, "Hey! There's a gigantic silkworm swimming in the water out there!"

The monster didn't even turn its head toward the tiny fishing boat. It merely continued to ride the waves as it went by, emitting its pale light. Occasionally, the crew thought they could hear it emit an odd groan, as if crying out.

Shin'ichi Chūjō kept his eyes fixed on the stage as he bit his lower lip. His assistant, Michiko Hanamura, had joined him in the adjacent seat, but she seemed a little perplexed. Since coming back from Infant Island, he had become a man of few words who spent long periods of time just sitting at his desk, deep in thought. Sometimes he flew into unexpected bouts of anger that really upset her, but now as he sat staring at the stage, biting his lip in disapproval, she found herself disgusted with him.

Everything was gorgeous. The voices of the four fairies kept a proper distance from the musical accompaniment, but no matter what kind of music was being played, they matched the rhythm nicely. It sounded as if the fairies were emitting some kind of supernatural harmony, as if they were the ones accompanying the music rather than the other way around. The effect on the audience was intoxicating. It was strange how naturally their harmonies flowed with the music, regardless of whether it had a jazz beat, a Latin rhythm, or a thick layer of orchestral strings.

The final act was an orchestral piece written for the fairies by an up-and-coming Japanese composer. Nelson had commissioned it for an enormous sum of money. The music was remarkably effective in the way that it layered together live and electronic music.

The performance ended. The audience clapped so loudly that their hands hurt, but then something strange happened. The fairies didn't stop singing. Chūjō held his opera glasses tight against his eyes as he stared at the expressions on their faces. Hanamura tried to get him moving by saying, "Say, it's going to get crowded. Shall we go?" but he didn't respond.

Chūjō had noticed something strange. The fairies seemed to be repeating a single word over and over.

Mo . . . . . th . . . . . ra . . . . .
Mo . . . . . th . . . . . ra . . . . .
Mo . . . . . th . . . . . ra . . . . .

Still looking through his opera glasses, he repeated, "*Mo . . . . . th . . . . . ra . . . . ., Mothra, Mothra . . .*"

When the orchestra conductor tried to alert the fairies to the fact that the music had already stopped, Chūjō, who was still peering through his opera glasses, noticed a mysteriously cheerful look come over the faces of the fairies, who until that point had been wearing rather glum expressions. Were they pleased that their work—or one day's worth of it, anyway—had ended? Maybe. But then again . . .

Chūjō found himself not knowing what to think.

"*Mo . . . . . th . . . . . ra . . . . .*" The fairies seemed to be calling out to something.

Much to Hanamura's surprise, Chūjō suddenly leapt up and dashed into the corridor without saying a thing. Walking against the flow of the departing crowd, he rushed down the hallway to the door that led to the greenroom; however, his attempts to gain entrance were in vain. The room was heavily guarded because both the Japanese prime minister and the Rosilican ambassador were in attendance that night.

Not long before, Japan had established a military alliance with Rosilica. Negotiations over the alliance provoked numerous protests both inside and around the Japanese Diet Building, but even so, the Japanese government pressed ahead and ratified the alliance without getting a sufficient level of approval from citizens. That's why a night at the theater had been arranged for the prime minister and Rosilican ambassador. The domestic situation had calmed down somewhat since the turmoil, but the hope was that if the prime minister and the ambassador got together and put in a public appearance at the theater, it might act as a gentle breeze, calming things even more.

In short, it wasn't a good moment for Chūjō to stop in. The bodyguard simply pushed him out, like it was the easiest thing in the world.

Far out to sea, Fukuda, the reporter, was listening with obvious irritation to the radio on the fishing boat. Actually, what he felt was far worse than simple irritation. As he lay there being bandaged by the crew, his feelings had escalated into something approaching outright anger. Not long ago, he had used the radio to inform the mainland about the kidnapping of the Airena—the four so-called fairies—but when it came to Mothra, the giant creature the crew had spotted at sea after picking him up, all he said was that the boat had encountered something that resembled a gigantic piece of driftwood floating at sea. Fukuda wasn't sure if the people at the newspaper bureau would believe him if he told them about Mothra or what had happened on Infant Island. He thought it best to go with Chūjō to consult Harada, the nuclear scientist. He couldn't submit a story to the news without talking to the members of the expedition team first. That's why he had sent in only an extremely simple report so far.

At that moment, the boat was heading toward an island that offered air service back to the Japanese mainland. Fukuda prayed the boat would reach its destination as quickly as possible.

Chūjō, however, found himself unable to wait for Fukuda's return. He summoned his resolve and went to the bureau of the *Japan Eastern News*. There, he was surprised to learn that the story about the "luminous fairies" was already being covered by a reporter from the arts and entertainment section. When something happens in society, it quickly gets turned into some sort of performative spectacle. Such things were hard to avoid. In fact, that night, between the Airena's songs, Nelson had sandwiched a line dance by the Atomic Girls—a dance troupe that had taken its name from the atomic bomb. Such were the ways of the world.

When Chūjō unfolded his newspaper the next day, he was greeted by a photo that showed the prime minister and the Rosilican ambassador shaking hands while the Airena stood next to a bottle of saké on a nearby table. The headlines spoke of the musical achievement of the luminous fairies, which was literally like nothing anyone had ever heard before. After the troubles surrounding the ratification of the military alliance, Japanese suspicion of the Rosilican government had continued to grow until people were questioning whether Japan could trust the rest of the world in general. The fairies, however, were neutral and unaffiliated with any government, so perhaps they might somehow help dissipate the tension.

The entire century had been one of politics, and in the contemporary world even the arts are used for political purposes. That is perhaps unavoidable. It seemed the fairies were destined to appear as little more than a garnish alongside nice bottles of saké in the banquets of high society.

Toward the bottom of the paper, there was a small article about the gigantic piece of driftwood floating in the Pacific. Another newspaper ran an article that simply described it as something of uncertain origin washed out to sea. At first, Chūjō read the articles without giving them much thought, but then something occurred to him. He felt as if he could hear the Airena's song echoing in his ears, "*Mo . . . . . th . . . . . ra . . . . ., Mo . . . . . th . . . . . ra . . . . .,*" over and over. The words seemed to contain a great deal of pathos, but it also felt as if the fairies were calling out in some supernatural way.

Chūjō rushed to the university, picked up Michiko Hanamura, and headed over to the physics classrooms where Professor Harada taught. The moment he saw Harada's face, he blurted out, "It's Mothra! Those articles must be about Mothra!"

In Harada's opinion, it didn't matter if the thing at sea was Mothra or some other monster. There wasn't anything they could do anyway. Might as well believe the article about the gigantic piece of driftwood. In the meantime, Chūjō could choose to believe what he wanted. There wasn't anything yet to explain conclusively what it was.

However, Harada was furious when he learned about Nelson's inhuman behavior. Clearly, Nelson didn't fear the wrath of the gods. Harada agreed with Chūjō's plan to call Nelson to arrange a meeting; however, when they tried, they were curtly refused. It wouldn't be easy to get in to see him. Plus, considering the political situation in Japan, the Rosilican embassy had recommended that Nelson hire a bodyguard, and that only made talking to him harder.

Not everyone was thrilled when they heard the luminous fairies sing. Among the music lovers of this country, there were some whose ears were sharp enough to detect the sadness in their song. Some who went to the opening night were left with a bad taste in their mouth. Some even used the words *cruel* and *tragic* to describe the show, questioning what on earth the hardheaded prime minister and the Rosilican ambassador were doing watching it in the first place. Some angrily protested that after the troubles surrounding the military alliance, the governments were mobilizing the performance as a means to establish a calmer relationship between nations.

As she sat beside Chūjō and Harada, listening to their conversation, Michiko Hanamura couldn't help feeling like something fishy was going on. Afterward, she quietly approached a male friend of hers who had served as a leader of the student protests and conveyed her concerns to him.

One, then two days passed.

Nelson used the same strategy that he'd employed when suppressing the results of the expedition for three months. He forbade any television coverage of the luminous fairies for the first five days but then gave exclusive coverage to a single network.

He also forbade interviews. This proved effective at drumming up even more interest and curiosity. Other TV stations that were angry about being left out in the cold started criticizing the show. Before long, public opinion had split into two camps.

In the wee hours of the night following the fourth day of the show, Chūjō was at home when he got a call from Haneda Airport. Fukuda, the reporter, was back. He wanted to go see Nelson as soon as possible, and he wanted Chūjō to go too. The light was starting to fill the sky over Tokyo as Nelson and Chūjō raced in their separate cars toward the hotel where Nelson and the fairies were staying.

At the same time, south of the Kantō Plain, far out to sea, a ship was plying the waters of the Pacific Ocean. It was the *President of Hikkurikaa,* owned by P Shipping. Something was showing up on its sensitive radar instruments—a strange white blotch. On the right side of the round radar screen it continued to grow bigger and bigger, until before long it occupied a long swatch from the top of the screen to the bottom.

An airplane happened to be flying overhead. The *President of Hikkurikaa* radioed to the plane to request that it check out the anomaly. In fact, the ship probably didn't need to radio in that request. The airplane had already spotted the anomaly earlier, when the sea started to change color with daybreak. Right away, they sent out their first radio warning. It wasn't long before it came into the ship's field of vision. It was an astounding yet perplexing sight—it looked like a series of low hills covered with snow, moving over the surface of the sea. Almost immediately the ship started to beat a retreat from it.

Mothra had grown extremely quickly. Perhaps *grown* wasn't exactly the right word; it had transformed into an enormous creature. Its moans echoed across the vast expanses of the sea, creeping toward shore. In its strange groans and moans, there seemed to be some hint of melancholy.

"Listen, Nelson! We're serious!"

"Chūjō, Fukuda, I take my hat off to both of you and your tremendous powers of imagination."

"You're not listening."

"You say a monster is coming to rescue my cute little fairies? Where's the proof? As of right now, you're the only person who's seen the monster, Fukuda—or, rather, you're the only person who *claims* to have seen it. Who knows if you really did? If, however, such a creature does really exist, then what the heck is it? Is there some scientific name for it?" Nelson paused and shrugged his shoulders. "I wouldn't know. I work in the arts as a promoter." Then he changed the subject. "It's early, but do you want a morning cocktail to chase away the bleariness? Maybe something bitter."

"What are you blabbering about? We're in a race against time!"

At that moment, Chūjō suddenly jumped to his feet. Fukuda was stunned, wondering if Chūjō was going to slug or attack Nelson somehow. However, Chūjō began repeating in a strangely quiet voice, "*Mo . . . . . th . . . . . ra . . . . ., Mo . . . . . th . . . . . ra . . . . .*"

Nelson and Fukuda were taken aback and flushed with surprise, but it didn't take long before they felt the color drain from their faces. In response to Chūjō's chanting, the caged fairies in the neighboring room also began to sing, "*Mo . . . . . th . . . . . ra . . . . ., Mo . . . . . th . . . . . ra . . . . ., Mo . . . . . th . . . . . ra . . . . .*" Their voices melded to form beautiful harmonies. They kept on repeating the word over and over, as if their song might never end.

Chūjō and Fukuda dashed out of the room. A couple of tough-looking thugs that Nelson had hired for security were asleep outside in the corridor. The room next door was locked, of course. The tough guys began to stir. However, perhaps out of resignation, Nelson pulled a key from his pocket and ushered Chūjō and Fukuda inside the room with the fairies.

Since returning from Infant Island, Chūjō had devoted himself to the tapes he had recorded, dissecting and researching the language of the island. He tried speaking first. The fairy who had saved him from the bloodsucking plant was the first to acknowledge him; then the four fairies acknowledged Fukuda. As Chūjō and Fukuda spoke, Nelson grew increasingly irritated.

"We want to help you. We want to return you to Infant Island. But Nelson says no."

"We understand. We will be rescued. We will return to the island. But . . ." Their song trailed off, not quite completing their thought.

"There are many people in this country that sympathize with you. Not just us."

"Thank you. We'll be rescued. But . . ."

"But what?"

"But we're sad that our rescue will bring so much trouble and misfortune to the people of this country."

"What do you mean 'trouble and misfortune'?"

"You heard right. Mothra . . . Mothra will be coming."

This was the first time they had heard the word *"Mo . . . . . th . . . . . ra . . . . ."* issuing from their mouths in context. There was something oddly unsettling yet beautiful about the word. As they said it, a deeply mournful expression came over the fairies' faces.

The first reports had reached the mainland. The airplane flew overhead while the *President of Hikkurikaa* continued to circle the monster at a distance. Meanwhile, Mothra paid them no attention. Both the plane and the ship were sending a continuous stream of messages over the radio.

"Huge kaiju in Pacific. Likely headed toward southern shore of Kantō region. Giant monster is a mystery. Unclear if it will go ashore. Coastal defense forces, be on alert for orders . . ."

• • •

An emergency session was convened in the National Diet. Chūjō, Fukuda, and even the nuclear scientist Harada were so overwhelmed by the onslaught of newspaper, radio, and TV reporters that when they received their summons to a meeting of the Cabinet, they were barely able to make it on time. Even though he was a reporter, Fukuda didn't even have the time to write the manuscript that he had risked his life to investigate. All morning the words *Mothra, Mothra, Mothra* seemed to be echoing everywhere, no matter where one went.

> *This breaking news just in. Just now, the government has issued an emergency directive regarding the mysterious animal. The news we are about to report is based on the latest reports from the First Coastal Defense Force.*
>
> (1) *The likelihood of the mysterious creature entering Tokyo Bay is very high.*
>
> (2) *In terms of morphology, the creature strongly resembles a silkworm. It is even larger than the Godzillas seen in the past, and it is believed to be more dangerous.*
>
> (3) *The creature is advancing extremely quickly, and investigations are currently under way to determine whether or not its body contains radioactive material.*
>
> (4) *In anticipation of the creature coming ashore, residents near the coast should immediately evacuate, following the orders of the First Coastal Defense Force.*
>
> (5) *In response to the clear and urgent threat of an invasion by this gigantic kaiju, the government is currently in preliminary discussions about whether it should activate its military alliance with the nation of Rosilica.*
>
> (6) *Henceforth, this giant kaiju will be referred to as "Mothra."*

Mothra didn't make land until after sunset. It came ashore at Shichirigahama Beach in Kamakura. It caused such a large tidal wave that for a moment the whole island of Enoshima was temporarily submerged.

Despite the emergency, Nelson insisted on proceeding with his show that night, not wanting to lose any more money than necessary. It doesn't matter what terrible events might be unfolding: there are always certain people who have free time on their hands and who want to experience something out of the ordinary, whatever that might be. In fact, the theater was full that night.

Nelson had hired a bunch of menacing goons to provide security for the theater. Early that day, Michiko Hanamura had quickly sounded the alarm and gathered a bunch of students who had come to the theater to protest. All day long they had been demonstrating at the theater, shouting "Give back the *shōjibin!*" and, in English, "*Nelson, go home!*" The Four Fairies Show was coming to an end. The tone of the four luminous fairies' song sounded completely different than even just a few days before.

"*Mo . . . . . th . . . . . ra . . . . ., Mo . . . . . th . . . . . ra . . . . .*"

After coming ashore at Shichirigahama, Mothra had crossed over the mountains of Inamuragasaki to the Great Buddha of Kamakura. As the four fairies sang its name, however, Mothra suddenly changed direction and sped out to sea once again.

That night, the destruction was limited to the city of Kamakura. Chūjō and Fukuda surmised this was because of a heartfelt entreaty by the Airena, who wanted Mothra to spare the country as much destruction as possible.

The following morning, the Rosilican embassy issued a statement.

"The nations of Japan and Rosilica have already concluded a treaty, currently in effect, to ensure mutual peace and security for both our countries. We believe that in such explicit, urgent circumstances as these, the treaty ought to be invoked. Moreover, reports have been circulating, based on reliable information, about the fact that this deplorable turn of events has to do with the personal private property of Mr. Peter Nelson, who is a Rosilican citizen. Therefore, as a freedom-loving nation that believes it is the right for individuals to own their own private property, we believe that the treaty should be invoked to uphold this fundamental principle. The 700th Fleet Division and the 500th Air Force Division will soon . . ." From there forward, the statement described the planned military deployment.

However, it wasn't long before Mothra headed back to land once again. When word reached town that the gigantic larva had landed again, there weren't very many demonstrators at the hotel yet, making it possible for two large cars to slip away from the back entrance. The cars were headed not for Haneda Airport but for an airstrip in the northern reaches of the Tokyo metropolis.

Mothra stretched out the joints of its eight massive legs and bent its extremely supple body forward as it scuttled with terrifying speed along the Keihin Expressway toward the heart of Tokyo. Neither bullets nor shells pierced its body. The damage was far less than anyone had expected. He proceeded down the highway, but it was only once he reached the vicinity of Kasumigaseki that he started to engage in any active way with the surrounding buildings.[1] As soon as his front end reached the Japanese Diet Building, he ceased moving. Meanwhile, large jets flew overhead.

Once halted, Mothra began to spew out threads of silk from what appeared to be silk glands inside his gigantic mouth, starting the three-stage transformation from silkworm into a pupa, then

---

1. Until now, no pronouns have revealed anything about Mothra's gender. For that reason, the translation has to this point used the gender-neutral "it." Suddenly Hotta introduces here the male pronoun *kare* (he). The male pronoun appears four times in this paragraph and the next.

into an adult.[2] Mothra spit out an astonishingly large amount of fibrous material, covering the tower and both wings of the Diet Building, creating a silken cocoon.

What a strange sight! Bathed in the light of the sun, each and every fiber of the cocoon glittered and shone right there in the very heart of the Japanese nation. The cocoon lay there completely motionless and quiet. With this transformation, the destruction came to a halt. The cocoon didn't make a single sound. As long as it remained still, there would be no more harm. Once night fell, it began to emit a pale, silvery glow.

The decision was made that an attack on the cocoon would resume once the night was over. As long as it didn't move it wouldn't cause any damage, but by this point the situation was no longer just about security but national pride as well.

Meanwhile, Chūjō and Fukuda had issued a joint statement explaining that the root cause of the situation was that Nelson had destroyed the peace of the tiny nation of Infant Island. Although frightened, some upset citizens nervously pushed their way to the cordon around the cocoon so that they were in plain view of it. All together, they raised their voices and shouted their concerns.

"We shouldn't do anything hasty!"

"Just let it be, and maybe it will eventually turn into a moth and fly away!"

"Rosilica shouldn't be interfering in the affairs of our country!"

Even though he hadn't suffered any damage personally, one resident who apparently lived in Itabashi Ward or thereabouts kept angrily shouting, "Thanks, but NO THANKS!"

On the other hand, the Rosilican embassy argued that it was imperative to destroy the cocoon right there in Tokyo before

---

2. At this point in the text, when the larva forms a cocoon, the male pronouns mysteriously disappear again, and no pronouns appear anywhere from here to the end of the novella.

it transformed into anything else. If the cocoon hatched into a moth, then the moth would surely go in search of the four fairies and attack the nation of Rosilica . . .

However, in consideration of public opinion, the Japanese government halted any direct intervention by the Rosilican military and instead gave them a degree of command over the Japanese forces. The military provided a heat-ray emitter, which was set up and deployed against the cocoon. The surface of the cocoon emitted dark red smoke before erupting into flame. Before long, the entire thing flared up and burned with an intense, scarlet hue.

This had the opposite of the intended effect. The abnormal heat accelerated the metamorphosis, and before long, the cocoon ruptured of its own accord. What emerged was a gigantic moth: Mothra had completed a final transformation, developing enormous wings that completely deflected the flames, heat, and surging heat ray.

Now that Mothra had assumed the form of a gigantic moth, she did exactly as people had predicted.[3] As she knocked jet airplanes out of the sky, gold powder sprinkled down from her wings, and once she reached Rosilica, she attacked its capital, New Wagon City. The greedy and wicked scoundrel Peter Nelson had insisted upon continuing his show there indefinitely, despite what had happened in Japan. The theater was in a part of town called Radio Center, where there were rows upon rows of skyscrapers.

Public opinion had erupted in Rosilica over the violence in the tiny nation of Infant Island. There were demonstrations in the capital. In fact, someone shot Nelson in a failed attempt on his life.

---

3. Popular discourse, both in Japan and America, has typically treated Mothra's final form as female. From this point on, this translation will follow that tradition and use *she/her* pronouns wherever English requires a pronoun or possessive. For more on Mothra's gender, see the Translator's Afterword.

Although Mothra had come to rescue the four luminous fairies, it was impossible for them to get very near one another because of the tremendous differences in their sizes—the fairies were so tiny, and Mothra was incredibly big and strong. A single flap of her wings would be enough to send the four little ones flying. It wasn't long before frustration mounted. Mothra grew enraged, and the results of this anger were catastrophic.

Chūjō, who understood the language of Infant Island, received an unexpected invitation from the Rosilican embassy to set sail for Rosilica. Mothra had blocked the airport by circling overhead, so boats were the only means to get there. It was decided that Fukuda would also accompany him. When Chūjō informed the embassy that he'd accept the invitation, he began speaking about reparations as he and Fukuda glared at the ambassador with cold eyes.

New Wagon City was little more than rubble by the time their ship arrived. The local authorities, who were completely overwhelmed, still had the four fairies in a cage. They were protecting them, they insisted.

Upon consultation with the four fairies, Chūjō and Fukuda arranged to have them brought to the airport, which Mothra had brought to a standstill. There, everyone waited quietly, standing by as the four fairies called out.

Mo . . . . . th . . . . . ra . . . . ., Mo . . . . . th . . . . . ra . . . . .
Mo . . . . . th . . . . . ra . . . . ., Mo . . . . . th . . . . . ra . . . . .
Mo . . . . . th . . . . . ra . . . . ., Mo . . . . . th . . . . . ra . . . . .
Mo . . . . . th . . . . . ra . . . . ., Mo . . . . . th . . . . . ra . . . . .

Their beautiful harmonies flowed through the rubble of New Wagon City, drifting on the air. Mothra had been spewing radiation in the middle of the capital.

As they gazed upon the ruins of the city, the four fairies began to weep. They hadn't wanted this to happen. Two of the world's most important cities had been destroyed, all because of the violent disturbances breaking the peace of tiny Infant Island. It should be noted, however, that the damage in Tokyo was relatively light compared to what happened in New Wagon City.

Mothra was waiting. The four fairies bid a forlorn farewell to Chūjō and Fukuda. They crawled up to Mothra's compound eyes and settled there among them, without causing her any discomfort at all.

Ships that had been dispatched to near Infant Island reported Mothra's safe arrival, but shortly after touching down she flew away again. Some time later, *IG4-Space Park*, an artificial satellite managed by the United Nations, was proceeding with tremendous speed through interstellar space. It confirmed that Mothra skimmed through the Andromeda Galaxy before entering another realm of space—some sort of anti-world. Sending a human-created satellite into the anti-world after her was well beyond mankind's capabilities.

If the peace of the tiny nation of Infant Island is violated again someday, who knows? Perhaps Mothra might return once again from the anti-world. For that reason, it would be a bad idea for people to go seek out the island. We shouldn't even discuss whether Infant Island even actually exists or not. However, rest assured! Mothra will be back! All three members of our collective—Shin'ichirō Nakamura, Takehiko Fukunaga, and Yoshie Hotta—solemnly stand by this assertion.

On the airplane back to Japan, Chūjō and Fukuda seemed strangely out of sorts. What they were thinking and hearing was so obvious that it hardly bears repeating here.

Finally, at one point Fukuda clapped his hand down onto Chūjō's shoulder, as if to interrupt his thoughts. "Things aren't going to be easy!" he said. "Taking such a good speaker and organizer as your wife might make things rough on you!"

"What are you talking about?"

"Gimme a break. Michiko! I'm talking about Michiko Hanamura!"

Translator's Afterword

Hatching Mothra

Jeffrey Angles

The moths are a very mysterious race . . .
imagine what a moth the size of a house might do!

—Hugh Lofting, *Doctor Dolittle's Garden* (1928)

In January 1961, the quirky novella *Hakkō yōsei to Mosura* (*The Luminous Fairies and Mothra*) appeared in *Shūkan asahi bessatsu* (*Asahi Weekly Supplement*), a mass-circulation weekly magazine that featured stories on popular subjects, current events, and entertainment. In many ways, the novella was an odd piece of writing—a sometimes serious, sometimes lighthearted mash-up of ideas, styles, and loosely related subplots that, perhaps some contemporary readers might feel, doesn't entirely congeal to form a single whole. Part of this had to do with the fact the novella wasn't the work of a single individual but a collaborative piece written by three people, Shin'ichirō Nakamura (1918–1997), Takehiko Fukunaga (1918–1979), and Yoshie Hotta (1918–1998), all of whom were prominent postwar authors, each with their own interests and ideas.

More important was the fact that the novella represented merely a rough outline of a story that Tōhō Studios had commissioned to develop into a film. From the start, the three authors were aware that the studio would rework whatever they had written, add and subtract details, and augment the story with Tōhō's particular brand of innovative special effects. For that reason, certain parts of the story, especially the final action scenes, were left quite sketchy, thus giving plenty of room for the filmmakers to work their visual magic. When the novella appeared in the *Asahi Weekly Supplement,* it did so with an explicit byline announcing that Tōhō was developing it into a film. In other words, this short piece of literature also doubled as an advertisement, drumming up attention and generating interest in the blockbuster film *Mosura* (*Mothra*) that would be released seven months later, in late July 1961.

Despite its various shortcomings and stiffness, there are reasons the novella is deserving of critical attention today. In its pages, the world got its first glimpse of Mothra, the gigantic moth that flitted its way through numerous sequels and reboots, earning the affection of millions of kaiju fans around the world and becoming one of the most beloved monsters of the twentieth century. Because the novella appeared in print right as the film was going into production, *The Luminous Fairies and Mothra* gives a behind-the-scenes peek at the original authors' vision for the story before screenwriter Shin'ichi Sekizawa (1920–1992), director Ishirō Honda (1911–1993), special effects director Eiji Tsuburaya (1901–1970), and the other forces at Tōhō Studios reshaped it into the film we see today. However, as this essay will argue, an equally important reason for paying attention to the novella today is that, when examined in detail, it provides an instructive glimpse into the concerns of Japanese intellectuals about their nation's place within the international order that had arisen during the early Cold War period. In addition, if one reads the novella against its sources of inspiration and the adaptations that it inspired, one sees a revealing example of the ways that images, media, and messages shift as they circulate across languages and continents, while responding to their own historical moment in time.

Godzilla to Mothra

To better understand what the authors were doing in creating this novella, one should begin by briefly considering Tōhō Studios' involvement with monster films. In early 1954, a producer named Tomoyuki Tanaka (1910–1997) from Tōhō was brainstorming in an airplane headed from Indonesia to Japan. The project he was working on about the participation of Japanese fighters in the Indonesian war of independence had just fallen through, so he was in desperate need of a film he could produce by year's end to replace the failed project. Reading a trade magazine on the flight, he encountered an article on the American blockbuster *The Beast from 20,000 Fathoms* (1953) about a radioactive monster who attacks New York. Over the years, Japanese film companies had made many movies about ghosts, demons, *yōkai,* and other supernatural creatures, but there had never been a Japanese film about a massive monster that comes ashore and wreaks havoc on Japanese cities. Still, Tanaka wondered if it was possible to recreate some of Hollywood's success in Japan. The fact that just two years before, in 1952, RKO had made a small fortune by re-releasing the 1933 film *King Kong* in America was not lost on Tanaka, and the 1953 film *The Beast from 20,000 Fathoms* had built upon that success, grossing more than five million dollars.

Even more important in the conception of the film was the fact that earlier in 1954 an unfortunate event involving radiation provoked nationwide panic throughout Japan. In March, the U.S. military conducted a highly secretive series of high-yield thermonuclear hydrogen-bomb tests known by the military code name Castle Bravo at Bikini Atoll in the Marshall Islands; however, an unlucky group of Japanese fishermen on a boat ironically named the *Dai-go Fukuryū-maru* (*Lucky Dragon No. 5*) happened to be nearby when the blast went off. All the crewmen immediately developed severe radiation sickness, and one of them, the radio operator, died within the year. As if this weren't shocking enough, a subsequent investigation revealed that much of the tuna hauled in from the Pacific on boats like the *Lucky Dragon* demonstrated high levels of radioactivity from the bomb tests. Even though the U.S. military assumed that the relative isolation of the Marshall Islands in a quiet part of the Pacific Ocean would insulate the rest of the world, the radiation released by every blast—each of which was many thousands of times stronger than the atomic bombs dropped on Hiroshima and Nagasaki—spread far and wide, poisoning fish caught hundreds and even thousands of kilometers away. When the Japanese learned that the fish in their markets might be radioactive, furor, fear, and protest gripped Japan. To Tanaka at Tōhō Studios, the prospect of creating a film about a radioactive monster who insisted upon coming ashore no matter how much the Japanese tried to stop it seemed like a natural means to give concrete form to the radiation-related anxieties sweeping the country at that moment.

Upon consulting with the studio, Tanaka gave this idea to the popular science fiction author Shigeru Kayama (1904–1975), who produced a script that director Ishirō Honda, special effects director Eiji Tsuburaya, and others released as the now iconic 1954 film *Gojira* (*Godzilla*).[1] Through its evocations of devastated neighborhoods and cities, the film reminded citizens of the horrors of the world war that had ended only nine years previously. At the same time, however, the story also reflected the fears of a population concerned that the Cold War could bring nuclear weapons and radiation raining down on Japan at any moment. *Godzilla* was a solemn, thoughtful film that struck a chord with many mature audience members, but the film also proved to have an additional appeal: children were immediately drawn to the scenes of the monster rampaging through Tokyo. Even though the writer Kayama admitted that he had created Godzilla to serve as a terrifying symbol of an awful weapon too overpowering to resist, he quickly realized that young audiences were fascinated, even entranced by the monster's mighty power.[2]

Thanks in part to this multivalent appeal, *Godzilla* was so successful that Tōhō immediately greenlit the sequel *Gojira no gyakushū* (*Godzilla Raids Again*) for release a few months later in mid-1955. The story was again written by Shigeru Kayama, who had drafted the screenplay for the first film, but the sequel directed by Motoyoshi Oda (1909–1973) didn't succeed nearly as well; it was also somber in tone, but it failed to hit the same cultural nerve. Even so, *Godzilla Raids Again* marked a turn in the history of Japanese monster cinema by featuring not just one monster but an exciting clash between two giant creatures—an idea reused in nearly all of Tōhō's subsequent Godzilla films. One of the most exciting moments of *Godzilla Raids Again* comes in a fight between Godzilla and the newcomer Anguirus, who grapple with one another on the grounds of Osaka Castle, summarily destroying it in the process. Some have seen *Godzilla Raids Again* as a cynical cash grab, but just as *Godzilla* embodied Japan's fears of radiation and nuclear weapons, *Godzilla Raids Again* could be interpreted as reflecting Japan's anxiety in the early Cold War period about being caught between two heavily armed, massive superpowers that could destroy the nation at any moment as part of their own struggle. It was all too clear to Japanese citizens that, because the U.S.–Japan Security Treaty of 1951 let the American military maintain bases throughout the Japanese archipelago, Japan would almost certainly be dragged into any conflict if Cold War tensions escalated. Heightening this anxiety was the fact that Japan felt like the Soviet Union was, in geographical terms, breathing down its neck. At the end of World War II, the USSR had seized the island of Sakhalin from Japan, as well as four other Kuril Islands known collectively in Japanese as the "Northern Territories" (*Hoppō ryōdo*), thus bringing the Soviet military within mere kilometers of the northern shore of Hokkaidō. Unease about Japan's precarious position with one kaiju-sized superpower in its territory and another breathing down its neck is a theme that would recur more explicitly in several Tōhō projects, including *Mothra*.

The poor revenues of the hastily produced *Godzilla Raids Again* led Tōhō to shelve its plans for additional Godzilla films for several years. In fact, it wasn't until seven years later in 1962 that Tōhō released the third Godzilla film, *Kingu Kongu tai Gojira* (*King Kong vs. Godzilla*), directed once again by Ishirō Honda, the director of the 1954 *Godzilla*. One guide to the films officially sanctioned by Tōhō Studios comments that this "light-hearted satire of the Japanese television industry," augmented by a "fight to end all fights" between "two of cinema's most iconic giant monsters," was far from the "previous film's sober reflection on the atomic age and humanity's endless cycle of violence."[3] Still, as film historians Steve Ryfle and Ed Godziszewski note, this "entertaining mash-up of corporate comedy and monster melee" sold 11.2 million seats in its first theatrical run, plus an additional 1.3 million in later re-releases, thus making it "the most highly attended live-action Japanese science fiction film of all time," grossing 352 million yen.[4] From that point onward through the 1960s and 1970s, Tōhō started producing Godzilla films at an increased clip at a rate of one movie every few years.

However, in the seven years between the disappointing 1955 performance of *Godzilla Raids Again* and the successful 1962 restart of the Godzilla franchise, Tōhō tried its hands at a handful of different types of monster films, experimenting with different plots and formulas to see what might resonate with audiences. In 1956, Tōhō found success with the film *Sora no dai kaijū Radon* (*Rodan*), which was directed by Ishirō Honda, based on a novella by Ken Kuronuma (1902–1985), and features a monster accidentally released by the work of coal miners in rural Kyūshū, the southwestern island that served as Japan's most important domestic source of coal until the mines were exhausted in the late twentieth century. Environmental messages had been present in latent form in Tōhō's first monster film *Godzilla,* which attributes the monster's anger to the nuclear destruction of its natural habitat, but *Rodan* marked a turning point in the history of kaiju film by pushing its messaging in a more explicit environmental direction. Early on, the work reminds us directly of the dangers of global climate change, and as the work progresses, one can read the enormous pterodactyl-like Rodan, who destroys cities with the powerful, hot winds released by its gigantic wings, as an early, prescient metaphor for fossil fuel–driven climate change, which continues to cause ever greater, more destructive atmospheric disturbances with each passing year.

After *Rodan,* Tōhō tried various projects that took them in untried directions. Kayama, who had drafted the first two Godzilla films, worked with Tōhō again to come up with the idea for the screenplay for the 1957 film *Chikyū bōeigun* (released in the United States as *The Mysterians* but more literally translated as "Earth Defense Force"), directed again by Ishirō Honda, about an unknown group of aliens who suddenly appear, intent on colonizing the Earth and interbreeding with Earth women. Tōhō and Ishirō Honda's next monster film, *Dai kaijū Baran* (*Varan the Unbelievable*) of 1958, once again emphasized that mankind, even with all its science, had only a cursory, incomplete understanding of the world. In this film, also based on the work of novelist Ken Kuronuma, entomologists traveling in remote, mountainous Japan are killed by a prehistoric reptilian monster who eventually turns its sights on more populated regions of the nation. The following year, Tōhō went in a completely different direction with the film *Nippon tanjō* (released in the United States as *The Three*

Treasures but more literally translated as "The Birth of Japan"), directed by Hiroshi Inagaki. This film tells a modernized version of Japan's myths about the creation of the world and the ancient founding of the nation. One of the most dramatic moments of the film involves a battle between the deity Susanō and the dragon Yamata no Orochi, which has multiple heads, each attached to a long, serpentine neck.

All the above-mentioned films featured the special effects of Eiji Tsuburaya, who had become an increasingly essential figure at Tōhō since the success of *Godzilla*. Indeed, audiences were impressed with many of these films, especially *Rodan* and *The Three Treasures*, but executives at Tōhō were already beginning to worry that relying too much on special effects would not be enough to keep capturing audience attention, especially as monster movies continued to proliferate. Tōhō recognized that in addition to catchy visuals, innovative and thought-provoking plots were essential for keeping audiences satisfied. So, producer Tomoyuki Tanaka decided to reach out in a completely new direction and call upon untapped talent to develop a different type of kaiju film.

Hatching Mothra

Late in the summer of 1960, Tanaka had a member of his production team, Hideyuki Shiino (1924–1976), reach out to the author Shin'ichirō Nakamura to ask him to consider drafting a story for a new monster film for Tōhō. In an essay recalling his involvement with the project, Nakamura noted that Tanaka decided to involve him because he feared films that were "only geared toward children" would not satisfy all viewers; instead, he "wanted to create films that would give a full serving of entertainment to adults too."[5] For that reason, he decided to call upon Nakamura, an author known for producing highbrow writing of the type known in Japan as "pure literature" (*jun bungaku*), in contrast to the kind of popular, easily accessible "literature for the masses" (*taishū bungaku*) produced by authors like Shigeru Kayama and Ken Kuronuma, who had generated the stories for Tōhō's earliest kaiju films.

Although he was at the height of his creative powers, Nakamura was, in many ways, a surprising choice, considering that none of his work up to that point had anything to do with science fiction or fantasy. If anything, Nakamura was known for his work in poetry and literary fiction, much of which dealt with the ideological struggles of intellectuals living through the oppressive years of World War II. Nakamura's understanding was that Tanaka hoped he would bring a bit of gravitas that could help attract attention. Interestingly, when the director Ishirō Honda talked about *Mothra* after the fact, he remembered the inception of the film in a different way, as an attempt to move some of the more somber monster films that Tōhō had been producing in a lighter direction. "'We wanted to do something that was new, for the whole family, like a Disney or Hollywood type of picture,' said Honda. 'We wanted it to be brighter, nicer.'"[6]

Born in Tokyo in 1918, Shin'ichirō Nakamura had lost his mother at a young age and spent his childhood with relatives in Shizuoka Prefecture. He eventually made his way back to Tokyo, where he attended the First Higher School, one of the most elite college prep schools in the nation. From there, he entered the prestigious Tokyo Imperial University, where he studied French literature and befriended a number of future critics and novelists who would mold the literary landscape of the 1930s. In 1942, Nakamura and a couple of other left-leaning yet nondoctrinaire aspiring writers—including future novelist Takehiko Fukunaga (another author of *The Luminous Fairies and Mothra* who will be discussed below)—founded a group called *Matinée Poétique* (*Machine poechiku*), dedicated to creating a new literature inspired by

Western poetic forms, even though borrowing from Western models during the most nationalistic, censorship-heavy years of World War II might not have seemed like the most natural choice. As Nakamura himself noted, the strong nationalistic orientation of the era gave him and his comembers a certain degree of intellectual freedom; cut off from the West and uninterested in the dominant trends in their own country, they strove to find their own way through the dark valley of the war years.[7] Later, as Japan emerged from the war and its strict censorship, this group continued its work, serving as a fresh, internationally minded force in Japanese poetry until 1950, when the various members moved apart and started working in other genres, especially fiction and criticism.

It was after Japan's 1945 surrender that Nakamura's work finally began to reach a wide audience. *Shi no kage no shita ni* (*Under the Shadow of Death*, 1947) explores the life of an author living through the Pacific War and doing his best to work under the system of heavy imperial censorship. This novel, which broke dramatically from the type of propaganda-laden fiction produced in imperial wartime Japan, established Nakamura as a major new voice in postwar literature; for the next few decades he continued to publish one major novel every couple of years. Several of his works from the 1950s portray the emotional and ideological struggles of intellectuals during and after the war, including two important novels, *Kokū no bara* (*Roses of Emptiness*) and *Kaiten mokuba* (*Wood Horses Going Round*), both published in 1957. The same year those novels came out, Nakamura's wife used sleeping pills to commit suicide, sending him into a downward spiral of depression that eventually led him to undergo electroconvulsive therapy.

Just as Nakamura was beginning to recover, the request came from Tōhō to work on the story for a new kaiju film. It wasn't Nakamura's first experience writing for the cinema. A few years earlier he had worked with producer Tomoyuki Tanaka, the producer behind *Godzilla*, as the principal screenwriter for the 1954 film version of Yukio Mishima's (1925–1970) classic modern romance *Shiosai* (*The Sound of Waves*). After that he wrote an original story that Shōchiku Studios would turn into the 1961 film *Netsuaisha* (*The Enraptured*). The Tōhō project, however, was an entirely different type of film, and Nakamura recalled that "as someone with a stronger-than-usual, mischievously childlike spirit," he leapt at the chance to write a piece of fantasy.[8] However, he called upon two of his close friends, the novelists Takehiko Fukunaga and Yoshie Hotta, to work on the story with him. It's not known exactly what Nakamura said to Tanaka at Tōhō to get him to agree to this plan, but in any case, it was decided that the three authors would divide the project between them. Nakamura would write the first part of the story, then pass it to Fukunaga to write the second part, who would then give it to Hotta for the conclusion.

Although it is unusual in the English-speaking world to find commercially published literature written by relay in this fashion, such collaborative literary projects were not unknown in Japan. For centuries, one of the most popular practices in the Japanese poetic world was the production of *renga,* sequences of linked poems in which one poet would write a verse and then pass to another poet for the next portion. In the twentieth century, magazines had sometimes applied a similar idea to fiction, creating a small subgenre of novels known in Japanese as *rensaku* (works written by relay), *gassaku shōsetsu* (collaborative novels), or in more modern times *rirē shōsetsu* (relay novels). This practice was most common not in highbrow literature but in genre fiction; editors commissioned such works in the hopes that the collaboration would unlock ideas more creative and playful than what any individual author might produce on their own, thus enriching genres that tended to get repetitious because of their very specificity.

For instance, in the 1930s the novelist Ranpo Edogawa (1894–1965), who holds a special place in literary history for producing some of the first distinctively Japanese detective fiction (and who modeled his unusual Japanese pen name, "Edogawa Ranpo" in the traditional Japanese order, after the American writer Edgar Allan Poe), produced a number of such works, which contributed significantly to popularizing the idea among editors. The most famous of these was a lighthearted detective novel titled *Egawa Ranko* written by six prominent crime novelists. As in many examples of the genre, the pleasure of reading the work comes in the surprising plot twists introduced by each subsequent author, but the text also includes a number of self-referential jokes designed to entertain readers. In this case, Ranpo Edogawa, the male lead author, worked in a figure inspired by himself—a female character named Ranko Egawa, which sounds strikingly like his own—thus creating a self-referential case of what one might call "literary drag." This practice of producing playful, collaborative novels, replete with in-house jokes and plays on the authors' own names, only grew in the postwar period, reaching its height in the late 1950s and 1960s, right when *The Luminous Fairies and Mothra* was being conceived.[9]

One of the friends Nakamura enlisted, Takehiko Fukunaga, had been an original member of *Matinée Poétique* with Nakamura. In the postwar period, Fukunaga had emerged as a strong-willed and ambitious novelist, who felt that Japan's "self-complacent, narrow-minded" writing had contributed to a dangerous attitude of Japanese exceptionalism.[10] As literary historian Donald Keene notes, Fukunaga viewed Japanese literature as "so absorbed by what was peculiarly Japanese" that it disregarded "the general human condition."[11] Fukunaga rejected some of the major trends of modern Japanese literature, such as the self-centered, comparatively realistic "I-novel" (*shi-shōsetsu*) that had been one of the dominant modes of literary production for decades. Instead, he advocated for the imagination of the author, which ought to reject doctrinaire explanations of human behavior and instead explore real-life psychology while avoiding clichéd stereotypes and state ideology. Of his novels, the one most widely still read today is his introspective 1954 novel *Kusa no hana* (*Flowers of Grass*), about a sensitive, seemingly bisexual young man's final years in a tuberculosis sanitarium. There he experiences romantic love for both a girl and her brother; meanwhile, he explores art and music and thinks about how these things might contribute to one's will to live in the face of almost certain death.[12] Throughout Fukunaga's novels from this period, one senses his antiauthoritarian, antidoctrinaire leanings. His eagerness to explore new territory may have helped make him attractive to Tanaka at Tōhō Studios, which was looking to create a monster film with emotions more complex than just panic and fear.

The other member of the Mothra team was Yoshie Hotta, who shot to national attention when he won the Akutagawa Prize, Japan's most prestigious award for emerging fiction writers. The award-winning work was the 1951 novel *Hiroba no kodoku* (*Solitude in the Public Square*), which explores the inner world of a young man living through a period of uncertain and shifting international politics while learning to question and accept the limitations of his identity as a Japanese citizen. Hotta had an especially international worldview: he had been living in Shanghai when World War II ended and only returned to Japan in 1947 after writing for the Chinese Nationalist Party. As cultural historian Michael Bourdaghs points out, Hotta threw himself into the cultural politics of the late 1950s and early 1960s, playing a key role in the Afro-Asian Writers Association (AAWA), which hosted a series of conferences that brought together writers from various corners of colonial empires to support the work of decolonization and to promote postcolonial cooperation across the globe.[13] In fact, Hotta helped to organize the first Asian Writers' Conference in 1956 in India, and in 1957 he published the book *Indo de kangaeta koto* (*My Thoughts from India*). This book makes it clear that Hotta identified strongly with the Bandung Movement, which emerged from the 1955 Asian-African Conference in Bandung, Indonesia, an important gathering of leaders from the colonized and decolonizing world who sought to create a nonaligned movement that would allow developing nations to chart their own path independent of the United States and the Soviet Union. After decades of organizing for the AAWA and publishing novels exploring the concerns of the developing world, in 1977 Hotta became one of three Japanese writers given the Lotus Prize for Literature, sometimes described as the "Third-World Nobel Prize." Given Hotta's support for the independent cultural and ideological development of an emerging Asia and Africa, it's unsurprising that *The Luminous Fairies and Mothra* would reflect concerns about the international order established in the early Cold War period.

To return to the tripartite nature of this novella, the reasons for Nakamura's decision to share the project with his friends are somewhat unclear. In an afterword appended to the 1994 reprinting of *The Luminous Fairies and Mothra,* Nakamura wrote that Fukunaga had been a "specialist" in film since his days as a student, and Hotta, with the success of the novel *Solitude in the Public Square,* had gained great popularity among politically oriented youth.[14] No doubt this helps to account for why he chose these two friends, but why bring on additional writers in the first place? Perhaps Nakamura felt he was in unfamiliar territory writing such fantastic fiction, so unlike the comparatively heavy, realistic novels he'd been writing until that point. Perhaps he was still struggling with his psychological health and didn't feel entirely up to undertaking the task on his own. Perhaps he felt overwhelmed by the time commitments he had already made to the Shōchiku film *Enraptured,* which was still in production. Perhaps he felt that working with two other writers would unleash fresh ideas that none of them could produce alone. Or, perhaps all these factors were involved.

In any case, the involvement of three authors meant that when finished, *The Luminous Fairies and Mothra* was, as mentioned above, a quirky text. The style of writing differs from section to section, as does the level of detail and even the principal areas of focus. For instance, the first section (Nakamura's) goes into great detail about the sights and sounds of Infant Island, but by the third section (Hotta's) the narration is surprisingly terse, especially in the denouement. Because the novella represented a guide for Tōhō as they started working on the film, the three authors focused more on the outlines of the story itself rather than the small details of how things might look or how the action scenes might unfold. This is especially true of the exciting scenes of Mothra's attack on Japan. Although contemporary fans might be surprised or even disappointed to find such scanty detail in the action scenes, many of which differ in important ways from the film, this lack of detail makes sense when one considers that Ishirō Honda and Eiji Tsuburaya had planned from the start to develop those scenes in whatever direction would work on the screen. At one point, the novella explicitly suggests that the story was a vehicle to generate excitement for the film in production. Near the end of Hotta's section, the authors break the fourth wall and address their audience directly to reassure readers, "Mothra will be back! All three members of our collective—Shin'ichirō Nakamura, Takehiko Fukunaga, and Yoshie Hotta—solemnly stand by this assertion."

Although the film was a blockbuster hit, it would be another thirty years before *The Luminous Fairies and Mothra* would be reprinted in book form.[15] None of the three authors included the novella in the editions of their complete works published during their lifetimes.[16] Perhaps this had to do with copyright issues; after all, it is more awkward to publish a text with three authors than simply one. More likely, however, is the prospect that the three thought of this tripartite project as somehow different from their single-authored work aimed squarely at highbrow adult audiences.

Even so, there are small details in the text that suggest the three authors did personally identify with the content and messages of the work. It is no coincidence that the names of the two main characters in the novella were created by recombining kanji characters from the authors' own names. The linguist Shin'ichi Chūjō's name (中条信一) borrows two of its four characters from the name of Shin'ichirō Nakamura (中村真一郎), the author of the first installment featuring this character. Although Chūjō is the main character for the first part of the novella, later the action focuses on the reporter Zen'ichirō Fukuda (福田善一郎), who breaks the news to the world about the terrible things happening behind the scenes. At first glance, Japanese readers would immediately recognize that Fukuda's name is created entirely out of recombined kanji characters from the authors' names—Shin'ichirō Nakamura (中村真一郎), Takehiko Fukunaga (福永武彦), and Yoshie Hotta (堀田善衛)—a hint that the character's actions reflect some aspect of the authors' inclinations, worldviews, and politics. Fukuda is, in a certain symbolic sense, a combination of all three of them.

Hatching Political Consciousness

So, what were the social and political issues that gave shape to *The Luminous Fairies and Mothra*? Answering that question requires a bit of historical background about the state in which Japan found itself in the postwar period. When World War II ended in 1945, only a decade and a half before the novella was written, Japan found itself under occupation by the victorious Allied powers, and American military bases were established in numerous locations throughout the country. In 1950 the American military began sending troops to a new war in Korea, and in September 1951 the United States paved the way for the end of the occupation of Japan by establishing the Treaty of San Francisco, signed by Japan and forty-seven other nations. That same day, the United States and Japan signed another bilateral agreement, the Security Treaty between the United States and Japan, which would serve as a de facto military alliance for years to come. This treaty allowed the American military to keep its bases in Japan even after the occupation ended and Japan took back its governance in 1952. In April 1952, 260,000 American servicemen remained in the country at 2,824 different sites, ensuring that Japan remained within the American military orbit.[17] However, the Security Treaty didn't explicitly promise that America would defend Japan even as Cold War tensions continued to mount. As mentioned earlier, in the mid-1950s the United States was developing the hydrogen bombs tested in the Marshall Islands; the Soviet Union responded by making its own bombs, creating an arms race that threatened to engulf the entire world. As the Cold War heated up, many peace-loving citizens in Japan who remembered the horrors of World War II were critical of the treaty, which stationed one of the superpowers in its own lands.

There were other criticisms of the 1951 Security Treaty. There was no timetable for the departure of the American military. The Japanese lacked an immediate mechanism to revise the treaty. Moreover, the Ryūkyū Islands, including the heavily populated island of Okinawa, were excluded from the treaty, essentially keeping them in a semicolonial state until their reversion to Japan in 1972. And because the American military was concerned that Japanese leftists might threaten domestic peace, the Security Treaty allowed the American military to quash any insurrections that might arise. The Japanese population felt that the treaty was so unbalanced that in September 1952 a poll in the *Asahi News* said that 40 percent of respondents sometimes thought Japan was not an independent country; only 18 percent of respondents thought Japan met the criteria to be considered independent.[18]

Although people of various political stripes objected to the treaty, leftists focused on its fundamental underlying principle: the assumption that Japan should side with the United States. Many felt that Japan did not need to align itself with one side or the other; instead, Japan could position itself as a neutral or unaligned nation. The Socialist Party charted one path forward with what it called in the years 1949 to 1951 its four "Principles of Peace": (1) making peace with Japan's neighbors on an individual basis, (2) avoiding bilateral military pacts, (3) forbidding foreign military bases on Japan soil, and (4) following the letter of the law by refusing to rearm, as described in Article 9 of the Japanese postwar constitution.[19]

Popular opposition to the Security Treaty grew in the 1950s, exacerbated by a number of incidents. In 1955, the American-run Tachikawa Air Base started an expansion into the village of Sunagawa, located in what is now Tachikawa, Tokyo, and this provoked huge and sometimes violent protests that continued into 1957. That same year an American soldier, William Girard, killed a Japanese housewife named Naka Sakai on a military firing range but was only sentenced for manslaughter, provoking renewed public fury at American troops. Finally, under the guidance of Prime Minister Nobusuke Kishi (1896–1987), negotiations for a new treaty started in 1958 and continued into 1959. The results aimed at greater parity: negotiators changed language that let the United States deploy its troops in Asia without consulting Japan, and they got rid of the clause that allowed American troops to be used against Japanese protesters. These revisions also stipulated mutual defense obligations and provided mechanisms for promoting trade and understanding. Last, the treaty specified a ten-year term after which it could be reconsidered, modified, or abandoned. Prime Minister Kishi and U.S. President Dwight Eisenhower signed the treaty in Washington, D.C., in January 1960, then sent it to their national legislatures to ratify. Meanwhile, the desire for Japanese neutrality had grown over the course of the 1950s. At the beginning of the decade, 22 percent supported neutrality, with 55 percent supporting the Japan–U.S. alliance. In 1953, support for neutrality grew to 38 percent while support for the alliance dropped to 35 percent. By 1959, 50 percent wanted neutrality and only 26 percent wanted the alliance. By the time the treaty was up for revision in 1960, 59 percent supported neutrality and only 14 percent expressed support for the military alliance.[20]

Riding this tide of popular sentiment, grassroots organizers, including many leftists, began planning strikes and events in advance of ratification. These protests, which swelled across the nation and eventually became some of the largest public demonstrations ever to be held in Japan, came to be known as the Anpo Protests (*Anpo tōsō*), taking their name from an abbreviated version of the Japanese word meaning "security treaty" (*Anzen hoshō jōyaku*). An organization called the People's Council to Stop the Revised Security Treaty (*Anpo jōyaku kaitei soshi kokumin kaigi*) served as an umbrella group, bringing together numerous grassroots citizen movements advocating labor rights, peace, antimilitarism, and nonalignment. When first formed in March 1959 the group had 134 affiliated organizations. A year later it had swelled to 1,633 organizations ranging from labor unions to politically minded artist movements such as poetry circles and theater troupes, thus demonstrating how widespread opposition to the treaty had become.[21]

As historian Nick Kapur points out, the Anpo Protests were motivated not only by distrust of the American military but also by a more fundamental desire to remain independent and nonaligned in the postwar international order.[22] Still, it didn't appear that Japan's ruling Liberal Democratic Party was willing to seriously consider nonalignment as an option. Eisenhower was set to visit Japan in June 1960, and the Liberal Democratic Party was pushing to ratify the revised treaty before his arrival. The Socialist Party, which controlled a third of the seats in the Japanese

Diet, had dragged out ratification of the treaty for months, thus putting it in peril. Worried about the deadline, on May 19, 1960, Prime Minister Kishi moved to defy parliamentary norms (and even some members of his own party) to extend the Diet session. When the Socialists staged a sit-in, Kishi called in the police and had them removed. When the opposition was gone, he called for a snap ratification in the Lower House of the Diet. The upshot: if the Upper House didn't vote on the treaty (an entirely likely outcome of this tumultuous turn of events), it would automatically take effect just in time for Eisenhower's visit.

These antidemocratic actions, which came to be known in Japan as the "May 19 Incident," provoked massive criticism, not just from political adversaries but also from Kishi's own party. The already large Anpo Protests swelled, taking up more and more space outside the National Diet Building, the American embassy, and the prime minister's official residence. On June 15, 1960, 6.4 million workers across the country went on strike in solidarity, causing the largest strike ever in Japan's history.[23] That same day, hundreds of thousands of people marched on the Diet Building but were met with violent protest from right-wing ultranationalist defenders, who attacked them with moving vehicles and handmade weapons. Also on that day, the radical leftist student group Zengakuren broke into the Diet and fought violently with the police, resulting in the death of a student from the University of Tokyo named Michiko Kanba (1937–1960). The response to this "June 15 Incident" was swift. Despite his angry and defiant attitude toward the protestors, Kishi resigned on June 16, and Eisenhower's visit was canceled.[24]

The largest protest of all, however, happened on June 18, when hundreds of thousands of people surrounded the National Diet Building, staying until the wee hours of the morning of June 19, when the treaty was set to go automatically into effect.[25] Ultimately, the massive strikes and protests of mid-1960, the largest that Japan had ever seen, did not stop the implementation of the revised Security Treaty, but they did force the nation to engage in deep soul-searching, asking itself whether or not the alignment with the U.S. military represented the best direction forward for Japan.

The Anpo Protests and Mothra

The events of mid-1960 were fresh in the minds of Nakamura, Fukunaga, and Hotta as they sat down just a few months later to write *The Luminous Fairies and Mothra*. In fact, much of the novella could be read as a critical reaction to the precarious international situation that gave rise to the Anpo Protests. Interestingly, in the novella the three authors do not distinguish between the two Cold War superpowers, but instead roll them together to form a fictional country called "Roshirika" (ロシリカ, rendered with the spelling "Rosilica" in this translation). Just as the authors created the names of the two protagonists out of the kanji in their own names, the authors created the name by combining the first two syllables of the katakana word "Russia" (*Ro-shi-a* ロシア) and the last two syllables of the word "America" (*A-me-ri-ka* アメリカ). In the film version, the name of the country has been slightly modified by reversing the order of the two middle katakana to become "Rorishika" (ロリシカ). Even so, it would have been obvious to Japanese audiences that the name was derived from those of the Cold War superpowers.

Inspired by the fact that the United States produced so many cars at the time, the authors named the Rosilican metropole "New Wagon City" in the novella, a play upon "New York City." However, during the production of the film, the decision was made to make the wordplay even more obvious by changing the town to "New Kirk City," which differs from its namesake by only two letters. Although several stories circulate as to why this change was made, it certainly strengthened the association with America. During preproduction, Tōhō had made a deal with Columbia Pictures, which had distributed some of Tōhō's earlier features abroad, for the rights to *Mothra*. To boost the appeal of the film to American viewers, the contract stipulated that the climax of the film should take place in an American-style city.[26] Even without the name change, however, the visual depictions of the city look far more distinctly American than Soviet. In fact, certain moments incorporate stock footage of the highways and shorelines of Los Angeles. Doing so was an inexpensive way to flesh out scenes, as budgets were running so high that the studio was looking for ways to conserve money wherever it could.[27]

So even though the superpower's name represents an amalgamation of Russia and America, it was the latter—the superpower that was in many respects closer in military, economic, and cultural terms to Japan—that loomed large in the imaginations of the authors and filmmakers. The section written by Yoshie Hotta, the most politically outspoken of the three authors, contains a passage telling readers that, even though America never is mentioned explicitly in the novella, something like the Anpo Protests had taken place in the world of the novella too.

> Not long before, Japan had established a military alliance with Rosilica. Negotiations over the alliance provoked numerous protests both inside and around the Japanese Diet Building, but even so, the Japanese government pressed ahead and ratified the alliance without getting a sufficient level of approval from citizens.

If one were to replace the word *Rosilica* with *America,* the sentence would accurately fit Japan's own experiences during the Anpo Protests just six months before. The mention of not getting a "sufficient level of approval" makes it clear that this is not a neutral statement; it echoes the feelings of the authors and numerous others who believed Kishi had acted antidemocratically by ramming the Security Treaty through the Diet. In the novella, the overly close, even subservient position on the part of the Japanese prime minister vis-à-vis the Rosilican authorities causes the protagonists discomfort, just as the relationship between Kishi and American politicians had caused anxiety among citizens wary of U.S. troops on Japanese soil.

To alleviate tension, the Japanese government in the novella tries to get the public to forget its antagonism through the use of soft power, namely the musical performance featuring the fairies, but the public also responds to that with protest. Chūjō's student helper, Michiko Hanamura, calls upon a friend involved in the student protest movements to gather university students to protest at the theater. When they do demonstrate, one of the phrases they use is "Nelson, go home!" (rendered in the novella as *Neruson, gō hōmu!* as if directed to an English speaker), an utterance that unambiguously echoes the rallying cry "Yankee, go home!" (*Yankī, gō hōmu!*) commonly heard during the Anpo Protests.[28] Further strengthening the connection between real-life politics and the world of the novella is the fact that the name of Chūjō's helper involved with the student activists is Michiko Hanamura—an obvious echo of the most famous martyr of Anpo-related violence, Michiko Kanba, the University of Tokyo student killed at the Diet Building on June 15, 1960.

Toning Down Politics

When adapting the novella into a film, Tōhō Studios modified many aspects of the story. One of the most noticeable changes is that the four fairies of the novella were reduced to two in the film, no doubt because the studio had found the perfect partner to work with: the popular singing duo The Peanuts, made up of identical twin sisters Yumi Itō (1941–2016) and Emi Itō (1941–2012). Plus, it was easier to create a sense of intimacy on screen with just two fairies rather than four. Another important change involved cutting the creation myth that explains Mothra's origins, which no doubt would have been difficult to film. Instead, the Tōhō production team replaced it with the discovery of a mysterious text in an unknown writing system, including a strange symbol that recurs later in the film and takes on a cross-cultural, quasi-religious symbolism, implying that Mothra is some sort of messianic savior—a move that Tōhō hoped might make the story more appealing to a crossover American market. Making an exhaustive list of all the other differences between novella and film is beyond the scope of this essay; plus, it would probably steal the fun from many *Mothra* fans who would enjoy making those comparisons on their own.[29] However, because it is directly relevant to the historical and political subtext of the film, I will focus on one of the biggest and most striking modifications: the decision to change the site where Mothra spins its cocoon.

In the third and sketchiest part of the novella (Hotta's contribution), the larva arrives in Japan at Shichirigahama Beach, near the picturesque island of Enoshima, a popular spot for summer tourists. There Mothra passes by numerous landmarks, including the iconic, monumental bronze statue of the Great Buddha located outdoors on the grounds of Kōtoku-in Temple. Hotta likely decided to include these famous landmarks for their visual appeal and their explicitly Japanese character, which might appeal to international viewers. Not coincidentally, these famous sites were also located just about five kilometers east of Hotta's own home in the seaside town of Zushi, where he had moved in 1948, so he had the added fun of bringing Mothra practically into his own backyard.

Shortly afterward, Mothra crawls back onto shore, this time

speeding into Tokyo and settling in front of the Diet Building in Kasumigaseki, the instantly recognizable building that serves as the legislative heart of the Japanese government. (This is the same building leveled at the height of Godzilla's destructive rampage in the 1954 film and where the government convenes an emergency session in the 1957 film *The Mysterians*. Also, in the 1962 film *King Kong vs. Godzilla*, the great ape scales this building in a scene clearly fashioned after the famous skyscraper scene in the classic American film from 1933.) Once the larva climbs on top of the National Diet Building, it stops its movements and weaves its cocoon. Meanwhile, a large crowd of upset citizens gathers outside the Diet Building, angrily protesting the international malfeasance that prompted this disastrous turn of events.

This scene was a clear callback to the massive Anpo Protests that had taken place in the same spot just months before. As in the student protest scene, some of the rallying cries of the novella's angry protestors, especially "Rosilica shouldn't be interfering in the affairs of our country!" and "Thanks, but NO THANKS!," echo the chants used during the real-life demonstrations. In his afterword to a 1994 reprint of the novella, Nakamura wrote about the authors' original hopes for this scene. In his recollections, he makes it perfectly clear that in his and the other authors' minds, when they were talking about the Rosilicans, they were really imagining the Americans with their strong military. Here is how they originally proposed that the scene unfold to the producer Tomoyuki Tanaka during a meeting in 1960.

> In order to get rid [of the larva on top of the Diet Building], the Japanese Self-Defense Forces would be deployed, but it was there that the three of us authors introduced into the story the U.S.–Japan Security Treaty. In accordance with the treaty, the Japanese government requests the deployment of the American military, which envelops the crowds of Anpo

protestors surrounding the Diet Building. Here, we were going to borrow some shots from news reels. At the United Nations headquarters in New York City, the Soviet Union would apply its veto power to stop the invoking of the Security Treaty, and there too, the scenes of tense dispute would continue. The screen would cut back and forth between the surroundings of the Diet Building in Tokyo and the UN conference rooms in New York with increasing speed, and as the excitement reached its peak, the cocoon would break open, and the moth would fly up from the summit of the Diet Building in the last scenes. This was my plan, but our producer Tanaka flatly rejected the plan with a single sentence: "That sounds like an independent production. . . ."[30]

Tanaka's comment about the authors' plan being an "independent production" alludes to a trend in the Japanese filmmaking industry at the time. After the end of the war, Tōhō became embroiled in a fierce labor dispute, and numerous people, especially those interested in making smaller, less profitable films that dealt with social issues, were dismissed. These filmmakers soon turned to making independent productions outside of the studio system; because they didn't have to obey the dictates of producers and funders, they could follow their own visions while bringing social messages to the screen. Without studio backing, these independent productions were less widely distributed, but quite a few have since been recognized as masterpieces that provide a valuable window into their moment in time. By saying that the three authors' original plan for the Mothra plotline sounded like an "independent production," Tanaka was telling the authors that their plan was too political and might harm ticket sales. Tōhō simply didn't want to evoke such explicit memories of the Anpo Protests.

The screenwriters and directors decided to cut the scenes set in Kamakura, thus conserving funds for what would be the more expensive scenes in New Kirk City, and simply bring Mothra directly into Tokyo. Rather than setting the stage at the Diet Building, however, the filmmakers decided to have Mothra crawl up Tokyo Tower instead. This building was brand-new, completed in 1958, and served as an important symbol of Tokyo's postwar reconstruction. Inspired by the Eiffel Tower, Tokyo Tower stood three meters taller than its Paris counterpart, making it the world's tallest freestanding tower at the time. Moreover, it had cleaner, less ornamented lines than the Eiffel Tower, thus positioning it as the Eiffel's distinctively mid-century modern descendent. By creating this structure, Tokyo was claiming its place in the annals of world architecture, showing that it had risen like a phoenix from the ashes of World War II. Because most of Tokyo was quite low to the ground, the new tower soared over the rest of the city. (Until 1963, Japan's Building Standard Law had established a fixed height limit of thirty-one meters for buildings, and so it wasn't until after this limit was abandoned in favor of a floor-area ratio that skyscrapers began to appear. The 147-meter Kasumigaseki Building, completed in 1968, is generally considered Tokyo's first skyscraper.[31]) This meant that in 1961, when the film *Mothra* was released, Tokyo Tower was visible from a long distance in every direction. Tōhō's decision to have the larva perch on it and snap it in half was, therefore, symbolic; Mothra's presence was quite literally destroying the newly rebuilt, thriving society of postwar Japan. Plus, this change of setting allowed for dramatic filmmaking.

Even though it might have looked good on screen, shifting the location away from the National Diet Building toned down the political subtext significantly. In the film, large crowds do gather around the cocoon-shrouded skeleton of the tower, but they seem rapt on looking at the kaiju and its cocoon rather than making any kind of political statement. Whereas the novella foregrounds the Security Treaty explicitly and describes the Anpo-like backlash it causes, the Japanese citizens gathered by Tokyo Tower in the film seem too preoccupied to protest, and when the superpower lends Japan the heat ray, the gathered crowds show no sign of being worried, angry, or upset by its deployment. In the novella, there is no real description of the heat ray, but the film uses the words "cutting-edge atomic heat-ray emitting-device" (*shin'ei genshi nessen hōshaki*) to describe it, thus explicitly identifying it as a nuclear device. During the real-life Anpo Protests, a major sticking point for many protesters was the suspicion that allowing the American military to maintain bases in Japan would open the door to nuclear weapons arriving on Japanese shores, a terrifying prospect to Japanese citizens who remembered the horrors of Hiroshima and Nagasaki. Despite the fact that this was a deeply troubling prospect for many Anpo Protestors, no one in the film expresses any concern about the new nuclear weapon on Japanese soil. When the weapon is deployed, of course, it doesn't work at all—if anything, it even speeds up Mothra's maturation. The film seems to be suggesting that American nuclear weapons wouldn't actually protect people from harm in the real world. In sum, the filmmakers discarded the callbacks to the real-life Anpo Protests and the Security Treaty, which they thought might hurt ticket sales, and instead underlined a less divisive theme with which most Japanese citizens already agreed—namely, that nuclear weapons are bad and only precipitate more problems.

Much like Yoshie Hotta, who wished that Japan would forge stronger ties with the decolonizing nations of the Pacific, Asia, and Africa instead of simply aligning itself with the United States, the characters in the novel seek to create a relationship between Japan and the oppressed people of Infant Island. In the novella, the main voices of conscience, Chūjō and Fukuda, do not side with Rosilica, which uses people like Nelson—self-involved, money-grubbing capitalists willing to ignore human rights for their own gain—to shape national and international policy. Instead, Chūjō and Fukuda's sympathies lie with the Infant Islanders, who suffer horrific, repeated injustices at the hands of the larger nation. In his detailed study of *Mothra,* cultural critic Shuntarō Ono notes that the novella carefully establishes the great lengths that Chūjō and Fukuda go to in order to master the language of the Infant Islanders. They do not expect the indigenous population to learn Japanese; instead, they choose to engage with the Infant Islanders by communicating in their own language, an attitude that suggests a desire to forge egalitarian bonds, regardless of level of technological development. (In the 1961 film, the descriptions of how Chūjō and Fukuda learn the indigenous language have been almost completely cut away.) Ono also observes that Chūjō holds a prestigious post as a linguist at a university while Fukuda works as a newspaper reporter, and so they both belong to fields dedicated to the production of truth: academia and journalism.[32] By having these two characters cooperate even as they work in their separate fields, the three authors reveal their idealistic belief that academia and journalism can work together to produce new types of unbiased knowledge that might help form bridges between the developed and developing worlds.

Interestingly, in the novella, Chūjō plays the primary role in the first section, and Fukuda emerges as an important character only later. When the novella was adapted into a film, a decision was made to promote Fukuda, as a journalistic investigator and concerned citizen, to a more central role, introducing him extremely early in the story, even before Chūjō, and having him accompany the first exploratory expedition to Infant Island. In doing so, the film emphasizes the central role of journalism in fighting for the rights of disadvantaged and oppressed people. As an aside, one might note that, while Fukuda uses his profession and wits to fight injustice, Tōhō wrote into the script a number of lighthearted scenes in which he goes undercover, sneaks into precarious situations, and even gets into silly-looking fights. Playing the role of Fukuda is the well-known comic actor Frankie Sakai (1929–1996), who brings an element of humor to what could otherwise be quite a ponderous story. In making these modifications and others, such as giving Chūjō a thirteen-year-old brother, Tōhō attempted to broaden the appeal of the story to younger audiences.

Considering that one of the central political messages of the novella was that Japan should identify with and support the citizens of small, endangered nations, it is worth saying a few words about the particular terms used to refer to the Infant Islanders. Some readers may rightly feel uncomfortable with the descriptions of the dark-skinned islanders. It is true that several words now considered non–politically correct do appear in the story; for instance, in the lead-up to the creation legend written by Takehiko Fukunaga in the middle part of the story, the pejorative word *mikaijin,* rendered as "uncivilized peoples" in this translation, appears once, not specifically in reference to the Infant Islanders but to developing people around the world. The main word used to refer to the Infant Islanders throughout the book is *genjūmin,* a term consisting of the characters meaning "original-inhabiting-people" (原住民), translated in this text as either "indigenous population" or "natives." When the novella was written, the word *genjūmin,* which is not intrinsically malicious, was relatively common in Japanese and was even used by politically aware and sensitive intellectuals. Still, it had been used to talk about people in colonial situations for so many years, often by people who looked down on colonized populations, that the word was eventually stained by association. Today, the preferred alternative is *senjūmin* (先住民, literally "before-inhabiting-people"), which is less tainted with colonial discourse.[33] In this way, the changing destiny of the Japanese word *genjūmin* parallels that of the English word *native,* which while not intrinsically discriminatory, in some cases carries echoes of the colonial past. In his study of *The Luminous Fairies and Mothra,* scholar Hiroya Yoshitani notes that a few very tiny seemingly typographical errors were fixed when the original 1961 edition was reprinted in 1994, but he observes one additional change that is somewhat more striking. In Fukunaga's section, the original text uses the word *dojin,* literally "dirt people" (土人), one time to refer to the indigenous population.[34] This word is now treated as openly discriminatory because it suggests that the people in question are simple, basic, of the earth, and perhaps even physically filthy. In the 1994 reprint released by the major publishing house Chikuma Shobō, the word was changed to *genjūmin* to erase the discriminatory overtones. At that point Fukunaga had passed away, so this edit was probably orchestrated by the editors or Nakamura, who was still living.

The fact that the word *dojin* appeared only once in the 1961 text and in a section dedicated to trying to understand the Infant Islanders implies that Fukunaga wasn't necessarily trying to be cruel. Even when authors have honest, liberal, or even liberatory intentions, they are products of their moment in history and may uncritically use the language that circulates in the society around them. From reading the novella, it seems clear that the three authors did not intend offense. If they had wanted to suggest that technologically less advanced populations in the colonial world were inferior, they no doubt would have used some of the many overtly pejorative words that were available—*yabajin* (barbarian), *banzoku* (barbarian tribe), *ban'i* (foreign savage), *dōmōjin* (savage person), *genshi-teki* (primitive), *ban'ya* (barbaric), or *soya* (rustic, boorish)—but nothing like them appear anywhere in the text. If anything, the text shows readers that the Infant Islanders are far more openhearted and environmentally savvy than their colonial Rosilican masters, who destroy the environment with nuclear weapons and murder large groups of people in cold blood for their own profit.

Why the Pacific?

Nakamura, Fukunaga, and Hotta wanted to write a story that showed Japanese viewers that, instead of aligning with superpowers, Japan had another route, namely empathizing with the developing and decolonizing world, serving them as an ally and perhaps even as a protector. However, to accomplish that goal, the authors could have set their story in any number of locations in Asia, Africa, or Central or South America. Why choose a Pacific island as a setting?

The Pacific was not only relatively close to Japan, it was already relatively familiar to the Japanese. In fact, large swaths of it had been incorporated into the Japanese Empire not long before. Take, for instance, the case of Micronesia. During World War I, Japan sided with the Allies against Germany, which controlled the majority of Micronesia, and so in 1914, Japan sent its navy to take over the German-controlled islands, which remained in Japanese hands until 1945. As the Great Depression settled over Japan in the 1930s and millions of people struggled to find work, moving to the colonies was one solution to the employment problem; as a result, the Japanese colonial population in Micronesia swelled from less than 20,000 in 1930 to 50,000 in 1935, and the local population quickly found itself a minority in many of its own cities.[35] A number of other Japanese colonies in Polynesia and Melanesia also attracted Japanese workers, quickly leading to a burgeoning colonial presence. Later, after the outbreak of the Pacific War, these colonists were joined by numerous Japanese soldiers and military vessels. Terrible battles ensued, and Japanese soldiers and colonists perished from starvation, suicide attacks, and malaria.

As the postwar period progressed and these memories faded in the minds of some, the association of the South Pacific and Japan's own colonial past gave way to another trope widely circulated in the mass media, which depicted the South Pacific as a simple, lush paradise suspended in an early moment in time. American popular culture was particularly influential in this regard. After the United States captured Japan's Pacific colonies, the region surged into the American cultural imagination, thanks in large part to the servicemen who had spent time there. For many American servicemen, the time in the Pacific brought about significant life changes. For instance, during World War II, the American writer James Michener had toured the Pacific as a member of the navy, and in 1947 he published a book inspired by these experiences called *Tales of the South Pacific*. Not only did the book win the Pulitzer Prize, it was quickly adapted into the smash musical hit *South Pacific*, which played on Broadway from 1949 to 1954, running for 1,925 performances.[36] The book was translated into Japanese in 1952, where it became a bestseller, with Michener traveling to Japan to promote it. In 1958, a movie adaptation filmed in Hawaii took America and Japan by storm, contributing to a rising craze for Pacific culture.

Around the same time, other sailors who had done tours of duty in the Pacific helped to create what came to be known as "tiki culture"—a loose-knit network of bars, restaurants, art studios, surf shacks, and other sites decorated with seemingly "exotic" visual touches culled from the cultures of Polynesia, Melanesia, Micronesia, Oceania, Okinawa, and even mainland Japan. Such places became fun, safe, and relatively affordable spots for ordinary Americans to go experience something outside of their everyday routines, helping the passion for the Pacific spill into the larger population. Once again, this culture was carried to Japan, taking root in GI-frequented bars. In 1959, Hawaii became the fiftieth state of the United States, significantly amplifying the fashion for tiki culture. Among the many films produced in Hollywood to capitalize on the fad for Hawaiiana were *Gidget Goes Hawaiian* starring Deborah Walley and *Blue Hawaii* starring Elvis Presley—both released in 1961, the same year Mothra was introduced to the world.

In the musical *Blue Hawaii,* Elvis capitalized on the popularity of Hawaiian sounds and dancing that had already become wildly popular in 1950s America. The profusion of popular songs influenced by Hawaii were exemplified by a craze for "hula songs," including "Hula Hop" by The Platters, "Bop-a-Hula" by Jimmy C. Newman, and "Lula Rock-a-Hula" by Teresa Brewer. Sometimes singers would even sing in the Hawaiian language, as in the popular "Hawaiian War Chant" performed by the Lennon Sisters and Larry Hooper. The South Pacific wasn't the only region that had made its mark on the popular music of the 1950s, however. Latin America, for instance, had left an especially large impression on the musical imagination of the 1950s with the cha-cha, the samba, the rumba, salsa, calypso, bossa nova, and other types of catchy dance music. These musical styles also blended with tiki culture, which seemed eager to bring into its fold any bright, fun music associated with island culture, whether it be from the Pacific or Caribbean. Before long, this music was playing not just in America but in Japan as well.

As international musical exchange picked up over the 1950s, these musical movements allowed Japanese consumers a small taste of international sophistication while imagining faraway tropical horizons. As scholar Yūjin Yaguchi has shown in his study of Hawaii's role in the Japanese cultural imagination, the 1950s were not easy for many Japanese, who were busy finding new ways to live in the postwar period while rebuilding society. Pacific-inspired films, musical styles, and dance crazes appealed to a population hungry for images of sunny climates and fun, carefree lives. It wasn't long before Japan began to respond with its own images of Hawaii, such as the film *Hawai chindōchū* (*On a Rare Path to Hawaii*), a Japanese comedy filmed on location. The story involves a Japanese woman who travels to Hawaii, encounters the Westernized culture of the Japanese-Americans there, and has fun learning about indigenous Hawaiian culture. The film presents Hawaii as having a friendly "aloha" mentality particularly welcoming to Japanese, who might go there to experience an exotic location, the grandeur of nature, and perhaps even learn to dance the hula.[37] Films like this, as well as stories from Japanese reporters and other cultural figures, reinforced the idea of Hawaii as a relaxed paradise that stood in stark contrast to the somber, work-filled environment of postwar Japan.

In reality, during the 1950s it was nearly impossible for most ordinary Japanese citizens to travel to places like Hawaii. Japanese yen were nearly impossible to exchange outside of the country, and it was equally difficult for ordinary people to get their hands on dollars in Japan because the government had taken control of the nation's scarce resources of international currency to ensure it had enough money for official and industrial purposes. Fearing that allowing mass travel abroad would mean depleting these reserves, Japan had limited international travel to people with official business—mostly athletes, cultural figures, performers, politicians, and reporters. It was only in April 1964, nearly twenty years after the end of World War II, that Japan officially ended these restrictions on the travel of ordinary people. During that year, Japan acceded to Article 8 of the International Money Fund agreement, which required a nation to terminate all restrictions on foreign exchange imposed for balance-of-payment purposes. At the beginning of the year, the Japanese Foreign Ministry estimated that 120,000 Japanese people would take advantage of the new freedom to travel, with about 50 percent going to the United States, with Hawaii the number-one destination. An article reporting on this in the *New York Times* stated that the United States had received 24,000 Japanese visitors in 1962, then 35,000 in 1963, but this number was poised to nearly double to 60,000 in 1964 as the new travel freedoms went into effect and more ordinary Japanese people stepped out into the world.[38] It is no coincidence that this shift in policy took place just months before Japan hosted the

Tokyo Summer Olympics, a project through which Japan sought to show the world that it had rejoined the international community.

Given that Pacific-inspired music and dance was so pervasive in the popular culture of the time, it is not surprising that Tōhō featured so much music and dance in *Mothra*. Nakamura, Fukunaga, and Hotta had carefully planted the seeds for the musical scenes in the novella, noting that the fairies' method of speech seemed "closer to singing" and drew in everyone who heard it. Later, Chūjō hears singing in Mothra's cave, and Nelson forces the fairies to sing to large audiences. When Akira Ifukube (1914–2006), the composer who had written the music for *Godzilla, The Three Treasures,* and some of the other early Tōhō monster films declined to write for *Mothra,* Tōhō hired Yūji Koseki (1909–1989), who had served as an in-house composer for Columbia Records. Drawing upon his previous experience touring Southeast Asia during the empire, he created a soundtrack full of tribal dances and other "exotic" moments, thus helping to establish what some have called the "fantastic mood" of the film.[39] However, the music contains a subtle political message as well. As Michael Bourdaghs has pointed out in his detailed analysis of *Mothra*'s music, the famous "Mosura no uta" (Mothra's Song) is first sung in Bahasa Indonesia and then later in Japanese, as if the barriers of language and cultural difference are simply falling away, bringing the singer and listener together in a temporary form of community.[40] It is no coincidence, Bourdaghs argues, that the song was sung first in Bahasa, the official language of Indonesia, considering that it was there that the Bandung Movement began in 1955—the same movement mentioned previously that sought to bring together members of the developing world as an alternative to aligning with the Cold War superpowers. In this way, the film's music serves as a reminder of the underlying message about political nonalignment.

Given the original authors' political intentions, it didn't make sense to tie the location of Infant Island to one specific place, but rather to create a "generic" island with an indeterminate location. For that reason, the novella gives little concrete hint as to where in the Pacific it was located. The passages about Infant Island being so irradiated by nuclear testing that it was believed to be uninhabitable were clearly inspired by the Marshall Islands in Micronesia, the site of the American military nuclear tests, but in the film, the hints about the island's location are contradictory. In the novella, Chūjō is identified as a linguist, but no specialty is ever mentioned; in the film, Fukuda mentions that Chūjō specializes in the languages of Polynesia, knowledge that would be helpful in communicating with the Infant Islanders. In the opening scenes of the film, however, when a member of the Japanese Coast Guard draws on a chalkboard to indicate where the ship *Gen'yō-maru* had disappeared, the location isn't anywhere near Polynesia. If anything, it is closer to the Philippines, somewhere north of Indonesia.[41] Later, though, in scenes that take place on Infant Island, one sees images of the stone *moai* heads on Rapa Nui (formerly known as Easter Island), located on the eastern side of the South Pacific Ocean, thousands of miles from the region shown on the chalkboard.

In interviews, the screenwriter Shin'ichi Sekizawa, who was in charge of rewriting the novella into a film script, admitted that in producing the film he drew inspiration from what he had seen in the South Pacific during his own military deployment in World War II. After being drafted in 1941 and spending some time in colonial Korea, Sekizawa was sent to Rabaul in New Britain and Bougainville in the Solomon Island chain, both located in the southwest Pacific. In fact, Sekizawa claimed that he came up with the idea that the kaiju should come from somewhere south, a direction never specifically identified in the novella.[42] Other members of the *Mothra* production crew had also been to Pacific Islands; for instance, even before the outbreak of the Pacific War, special effects director Eiji Tsuburaya had traveled on a naval vessel to Hong Kong, Singapore, Australia, Hawaii, and Saipan while shooting his 1936 propaganda film *Kōho sanman-ri, sekidō o koete* (*Across the Equator*), and this seems to have influenced his visions for the sets.

The point is that in designing the sets, backgrounds, and music for the Infant Island scenes, the filmmakers did something similar to what the creators of tiki culture in America had done: they pulled together elements culled from their own experiences and combined them with the kinds of "exotic" images of the Pacific common in popular culture to produce something intriguing and attractive enough to market to viewers. Indeed, there are lots of connections to different corners of the Pacific, both real and imagined. One sees red hibiscus flowers in the dancing girls' hair, much as one would find in the French painter Paul Gauguin's paintings of Tahiti or the popular Hawaiian movies from the time. The dances themselves seem like a combination of moves inspired by Hawaiian hula, Indonesian kecak, Māori hakka, and midcentury modern avant-garde dance. The music draws upon the drum-filled, dance-loving "exotica" so popular in the 1950s, while the use of Bahasa Indonesia in the lyrics of the famous "Song of Mothra" added to the international atmosphere. In short, the depictions of Infant Island fit perfectly within the realm of tiki culture, which in the words of one commentator consisted of "free-form interpretations of several island styles, mixed with a good dose of cartoon whimsy and a dash of modern art."[43]

Not all aspects of the depiction of Infant Island have weathered well. Contemporary viewers sometimes cringe at the dark makeup used to blacken the skins of the Japanese actors playing the Infant Islanders. Some of the facial expressions and behavior make the Infant Islanders look like throwbacks to an early stage of human evolution rather than contemporary *Homo sapiens,* which of course all living human beings are. Here, one senses the uncomfortable double-sidedness that one finds in many acts of mimicry depicting colonized people. When a person from a powerful culture imitates that of another, it can signal some respect, interest, or attraction to their culture; yet by enacting difference in visible, clear, and identifiable ways, the act of mimicry also simultaneously establishes distance, drawing attention to perceived ethnic or racial gaps.[44]

Historian Yoshikuni Igarashi has convincingly argued that the depictions of the Infant Islanders in the *Mothra* films "enact and package Japan's colonial fantasies for easy consumption" while simultaneously serving as an imagined alternative to contemporary Japan, where people were surrounded by a capitalist culture of hard work and consumerism.[45] Literary historian Robert Tierney has pointed out that since the nineteenth century, Japanese writing about the Pacific islands did not always depict those places and cultures realistically but often used them as a way of thinking through the experiences of Japan itself. In other words, the islands of the Pacific were sometimes presented as a kind of "alter ego" to Japan—places that might manifest some similarities to Japanese society while differing in other, significant ways. By writing about the Pacific, Japanese authors could "critique their own society in a veiled way, confess their own ambivalences, explore their experiences of modernity, or otherwise construct an imaginary terrain to write about themselves."[46]

It is no coincidence that the three authors of the novella named the island *Infanto-tō,* using the Japanese transliteration of the English word *infant.* The island's inhabitants are suspended in time, existing in a prolonged state of early civilization until interrupted by intrusions of the outside world.[47] In the film, the Infant Islanders are portrayed like the natives in tiki culture—sometimes infantile, sometimes humorous, sometimes threatening, sometimes eroticized, but always rather simple. One should remember that this is the work of the filmmakers; in the novella, by contrast, the Infant Islanders are never presented as anything other than noble and kind, existing in harmony with their environment even as it is under severe and brutal attack from the outside world. The

Japanese characters see in their simple nobility a mirror of what Japan could be, and so they respond by serving as de facto allies. One might criticize the historical amnesia of the writers, who seem to overlook Japan's own colonial past in the Pacific islands. That would not be wrong, but *The Luminous Fairies and Mothra* does demonstrate a clear attempt to overcome that colonial past by forming new alliances of support. The novella clearly reminds readers that people with power and conscience have a moral obligation to open their ears and listen to people in vulnerable positions, even if their populations are small and their languages unfamiliar. It is only by working on behalf of those others that the protagonists of the novella start the process of disentangling systems of oppression, and in the process, save the world for everyone.

Mothra as Moth and Mother

At this point, it's worth raising a question that's probably been on the minds of at least some readers of this book. Why might the three authors have chosen to make the central kaiju in their novella a gigantic moth—a creature that might, at first glance, seem relatively innocuous and not especially threatening or scary?

In his afterword to the 1994 reprint of the novella, Nakamura wrote that when he was approached by Tōhō about creating a monster movie, he thought it would be interesting to have the kaiju at the heart of the story undergo a metamorphosis on screen over the course of the film. In thinking about different animals that might allow him to do this, he came up with the idea of using a moth, since they go through multiple transformations over the course of their lives: egg, larva, cocoon, and moth.[48] This was a brilliant idea, since of course it would allow Tsuburaya's team at Tōhō to use a series of entertaining special effects to depict the life cycle of a single kaiju, with the final colorful moth being the most dramatic and visually appealing of all—perfect for the climax of the film.

In his study of Mothra, Shuntarō Ono points out that at least one of these stages, that of the larva, has a deep significance within Japanese society. Noting that the novella describes the larva as looking like a gigantic "silkworm" as it swims across the Pacific Ocean, Ono points out that silkworms and sericulture have deep connections to Japan and the modernization of its economy. Through at least the early part of the twentieth century, it was common for country homes to rear silkworm cocoons as a relatively easy way to make extra money. The cocoons they produced were then boiled (killing the silkworm inside), unraveled, and spun to produce thread, which was then woven to form silk cloth, a luxury item that could be sold around the world. Given this, Ono sees the image of silkworms and silk moths as deeply connected to Japanese culture and thus appropriate for a new, different type of kaiju, completely unlike those inspired by midcentury Western monster movies. He also notes that when Fukuda first encounters the four fairies in the novella, they are seated and weaving in front of the shrine where Mothra's egg resides, thus establishing a suggestive link between thread, cloth, and civilization.[49] However, even if Nakamura, Fukunaga, and Hotta intended this connection, it was severed when the story was rewritten as a film script and the connection with weaving was discarded. Moreover, on screen, Mothra is depicted not as the kind of fuzzy, white, small moth that silkworms turn into but a colorful, spotted moth, rather like a luna moth or other moths in the Saturniid family. Because creating an attractive visual spectacle on screen was paramount for the filmmakers, one can easily understand why making Mothra look like an unexciting white silk moth would not be especially appealing.

Although he didn't seem to recall exactly, Nakamura said it was probably Tomoyuki Tanaka who named the kaiju Mothra, bringing together the English word *moth* with the final suffix *ra* from the name of Godzilla (*Gojira* in Japanese), another member of the same fictional universe.[50] (Although Godzilla does not appear in *The Luminous Fairies and Mothra* or in the film based upon it, a statement issued by the government in Hotta's part of the novella describes the larva as "even larger than the Godzillas seen in the past." This single line of text makes it clear that right from the start the three authors and Tōhō imagined Mothra to exist in the same world as the 1954 *Godzilla* and the 1955 sequel *Godzilla Raids Again.* Just a few years after the film *Mothra,* Godzilla and Mothra would appear together for the first time in the appropriately named 1964 film *Mosura tai Gojira* [*Mothra vs. Godzilla*].) When writing the first Godzilla films, the name *Gojira* had been created by combining the Japanese words for two enormous animals: *gorira,* meaning "gorilla," and *kujira,* meaning "whale." Mothra was the second of the monsters in Tōhō's kaiju universe to use the *ra* suffix, but certainly not the last. Over the decades, Tōhō would reuse this same suffix, albeit spelled in slightly different ways in the English romanization, with numerous other monsters, including Dogora, King Ghidorah, and Hedorah.

Although Mothra's name is most closely related to the English word *moth,* many commentators have noted that the name also sounds like the English word *mother.* Certainly, the three authors of the novella created Mothra to be a profoundly protective, perhaps even motherly figure, determined to protect the fairies. Moreover, in the subtitles to the first English release of the film, Mothra is described with the pronoun *she,* cementing Mothra as female in the international imagination. For instance, film critic Jason Barr, who has written astutely about many Tōhō productions in *The Kaiju Film,* draws attention to Mothra's simultaneously protective yet destructive qualities:

> Mothra retaliates: she has, since her inception, been repeatedly tasked to "protect" Japan from invaders seeking to

> influence or victimize the country. . . . In her trail of destruction of city skylines, it is important to remember that such city centers represent capitalism as well, and Mothra's destruction of cities—even when it is incidental or provoked—fits well within her mystique.[51]

This view of Mothra as a motherly, mystical figure with strong protective urges yet a willingness to engage in violence when necessary, is justifiable, especially considering the gendered language in the English subtitles and popular discourse. Fans have often written about Godzilla and Mothra, especially as they manifest in films from *Mothra vs. Godzilla* onward, as a yin-yang, dichotomous pair, with Godzilla representing a strong, masculine, destructive force and Mothra representing a gentler, feminine, protective force.[52]

In the novella, however, there is some ambiguity around Mothra's gender. Japanese does not require speakers to use pronouns. Although pronouns do exist, they are used far less than in English, and in fact, it is possible to write entire novels without ever using one at all. If a subject is clear from context, Japanese typically leaves out a pronoun, but if context doesn't make the subject clear, writers will reintroduce the subject by name to reduce ambiguity, thus avoiding gendered language altogether. Plus, Japanese doesn't have explicitly gendered possessives, such as "his" or "hers," which might give a clue about a character's gender. Until fairly late in the third and final section of the novella, no pronouns whatsoever are used to refer to Mothra, and so until that moment, this translation has used the gender-ambiguous word "it" whenever the English language calls for a pronoun. My hope was that the use of "it" would not be especially jarring for English readers, considering that Mothra is in egg or larval form during those parts of the novella. However, when Mothra begins spinning a cocoon on top of the National Diet Building, the masculine pronoun *kare* ("he / him") suddenly appears. In the original Japanese, this word is used four times over a few consecutive sentences before all pronouns disappear again.[53] Although no gendered pronouns occur anywhere between the last instance of *kare* and the end of the novella, I have followed the tradition established in popular discourse and used female pronouns when talking about Mothra's final form as a moth. The notion that gender binaries are not absolute does have earlier precedent in the novella in the portion about the Infant Island creation myth. When the god Ajima breaks his own body in half, one half becomes the goddess Ajigo, suggesting that even male bodies have some latent element of femininity somewhere inside of them that can be brought out through physical transformation.

My decision as a translator to highlight rather than whitewash over the use of male pronouns, which appear for just a couple of sentences before Mothra undergoes the next and final transformation, may seem odd to some, but one goal of this project is to showcase for readers some of the most interesting and surprising elements present in the novella before Tōhō adapted it into the now famous film. One should remember that Nakamura wanted his kaiju to undergo a transformation. Considering this, the switch to and from male pronouns takes on new resonance. One might even read Mothra as a nonbinary or transgender kaiju, going through multiple stages in life before reaching a final, beautiful stage that represents Mothra's full, strongest, most powerful self. As a queer translator deeply supportive of my transgender friends, colleagues, and family members, I believe that in these small textual details of the original novella we find a story of change, transformation, and becoming that takes on special resonance today. In our contemporary world in which transgender bodies and identities are all too often subjected to severe and vicious attacks, I hope that Mothra's transformation into a powerful, beautiful figure that transcends limited binary notions of gender can provide a least a modicum of inspiration and comfort to some readers.

Doctor Dolittle in Infant Island

Although the extant scholarship on Mothra both in Japanese and English doesn't seem to have noticed this connection at all, it is nearly impossible to believe that significant chunks of Mothra weren't inspired by the famous children's book series about Doctor Dolittle, originally written in English by Hugh Lofting and translated into Japanese by the prominent novelist Masuji Ibuse. Because this connection has so much to do with the content and ideology of the story, this section will explore that linkage in some detail.

Lofting started publishing his Doctor Dolittle series in the 1920s. The books became so enormously popular in the English-speaking world that he continued publishing them through the 1950s, producing more than a dozen volumes, three of which feature a massive moth the size of a house, able to fly across vast portions of the Earth and even into outer space, just like in the final scenes of *The Luminous Fairies and Mothra*. Lofting's fanciful series was designed to be entertaining and funny for young readers, but they also sought to instill a sense of respect and curiosity about the natural world. Doctor Dolittle is not only a medical doctor; he is, like Chūjō, a linguist. Intent on communicating with animals, he studies the languages of the world's various creatures as he travels the planet learning from different types of fauna. A major theme of the book series is that even though animals all have different sizes, appearances, and life-spans, all creatures, even small ones such as crickets, bugs, maggots, and moths, have value and deserve respect. For instance, in *Doctor Dolittle's Garden*, published in English in 1927, the title character delivers the following message to his young assistant, Stubbins.

> Just now Man is on top as the tyrant. He dictates to the animal kingdom. But many of his lesser brothers suffer in that dictation. What I would like to see—and indeed it is my one

ambition as a constructive naturalist—would be happy balance. I've never met any species, Stubbins, that did not do some good—general good—along with the harm. . . . By making them our friends we ought to be able to get together and improve conditions all around, instead of making war on one another. War gets us nowhere.[54]

This moral about the importance of valuing the lives of creatures smaller than oneself has obvious parallels in *The Luminous Fairies and Mothra,* where Chūjō and Fukuda argue that the tiny fairies and hidden Infant Islanders deserve to be respected and treated as subjects in their own right. Doctor Dolittle argues that the hierarchical, self-centered thinking implicit in the anthropocentric assumption that places humans at the center of the world leads to war and conflict, much as some characters in the novella recognize that hierarchical, self-centered thinking on the part of superpowers allows for colonial exploitation, conflict, and even genocide.

In the passage above and many others throughout Lofting's series, one sees the author's dedication to pacifism and egalitarianism. Lofting began writing the Doctor Dolittle stories to his children in letters when he was in the trenches, fighting in the Irish Guard for the British army in World War I, where he witnessed the horrors inflicted not just on mankind but also on their animal companions. Lofting was severely wounded by shrapnel in his leg, and after being released from the military for medical reasons, he emigrated to America, where he spent the rest of his life. His own horrifying experiences as a soldier had taught him about the foolhardiness of armed conflict, which became a central theme in his work.[55] Lofting went on to become one of a generation of writers like A. A. Milne and C. S. Lewis who drew upon their experiences in World War I to write a new type of children's literature that attempted to sow ideological seeds that might one day grow into a more peaceful world. He once said, "If we make children see that all races, given equal physical and mental chance for development, have about the same batting averages of good and bad, we shall have laid another very substantial foundation stone in the edifice of peace and internationalism."[56]

It was precisely because of these values, expressed so strongly in his novels, that his books appealed to the first writers in Japan to encounter them. The first entry in the Doctor Dolittle series, *The Story of Doctor Dolittle* (1920), was published in Japanese in 1941, just months before the bombing of Pearl Harbor, which brought the United States into the Pacific War. A young author by the name of Momoko Ishii, who would later become one of the most prominent translators of children's literature into Japanese, had received a copy from an American friend some years before. Even though Japan's war in China had escalated and nationalism was infecting every aspect of the publishing world, Ishii decided to translate the book, hoping to share its peaceful, idealistic messages with children. She recognized that the propaganda-laden writing being produced at the time wasn't exactly what children were interested in reading. With the help of some friends, she started a small self-supported press called Bairin Shōnenkan, and *The Story of Doctor Dolittle* was the second book she chose to publish.[57] She did a draft of the story and turned it over to her friend and neighbor, the well-established novelist Masuji Ibuse, to fix it however he wanted. His brushup was so thorough, charming, and well done that she hoped he would do more in the series, but she came under pressure from authorities, and Bairin Shōnenkan stopped publishing immediately afterward. Unfortunately, because the book came out from a small publisher in a difficult time, it didn't reach many readers, but it did earn admiration from progressive thinkers. One of Ishii's friends, the writer and historian Shū Mizusawa, later wrote that the work which Ishii did "under the system of wartime Japan was nothing short of a miracle."[58]

After the war ended, Ishii began working with the influential publishing house Iwanami Shoten, and in 1950 she founded the "Iwanami Children's Library" imprint (*Iwanami shōnen bunko*), which strove to publish attractive and fun books that would contribute to children's intellectual enrichment. For the first four years of the imprint's existence, Ishii took the lead in scouting out new books for the series, and once again she turned to Doctor Dolittle. In 1951 Ishii republished the 1941 translation of *The Story of Doctor Dolittle,* and in 1952 she published three more books from the series, all translated by Masuji Ibuse, who was working alone this time. The volumes continued to come out one by one, and then during 1961 and 1962 those translations were rereleased with a few final volumes to complete the twelve-volume set *Doritoru sensei monogatari zenshū* (*The Complete Doctor Dolittle Tales*), all in Ibuse's translation. The fact that these postwar translations all came out from Iwanami Shoten, an influential publisher with good distribution, meant that the series now reached every corner of the country. Moreover, the positive, peaceful messages about the value and beauty of all types of life struck a chord in a nation still recovering from the devastating and catastrophic war less than a generation before. Parents everywhere bought the books for their children, leading the series to reach stratospheric levels of popularity.[59] As a result, Doctor Dolittle was very well known in Japan by the time that Nakamura, Fukunaga, and Hotta sat down to write their novella for Tōhō.

Masuji Ibuse, the skilled author who translated Doctor Dolittle, was the perfect person for the job, and his flair for style was one of the reasons that the book was so successful. Ibuse lived from 1898 to 1993, making him one generation older than the three authors of *The Luminous Fairies and Mothra,* all three of whom were born in 1918. Ibuse was a prolific author who quickly rose to prominence in the literary world. In 1938, he cemented his growing fame by winning the Naoki Prize, Japan's highest award for popular fiction. During the war and into the postwar period he continued to write prolifically, producing novels that were made into films and that won major prizes, thus ensuring his work was in the public eye right when Nakamura, Fukunaga, and Hotta were debuting. Unlike Hotta, Ibuse had a strong aversion to direct involvement in politics, but even so, he did explore themes that were dear to the hearts of the next generation of progressive writers, ensuring that they knew his work. For instance, Ibuse's strong antimilitarist feelings appear in his Yomiuri Prize–winning 1949 novel *Honjitsu kyūshin* (*No Consulations Today*), and one sees his terrible aversion to the horrifying power of the atomic bomb in the 1951 story "Kakitsubata" (The Crazy Iris), as well as his 1966 masterpiece *Kuroi ame* (*Black Rain*), which depicts the Hiroshima bombing and its emotional aftermath in hair-raising detail.

The reason all of this is relevant is that three of the Doctor Dolittle books—namely *Doctor Dolittle's Garden* (1927), *Doctor Dolittle in the Moon* (1928), and *Doctor Dolittle's Return* (1933), which for the sake of convenience I will refer to as the "moon trilogy"—feature many plot elements and images that also recur in the Mothra story, suggesting a strong line of influence connecting Hugh Lofting to the authors of *The Luminous Fairies and Mothra.* Of these plot elements, the most telling is the appearance of a character called Jamaro Bumblelily, a gigantic, benevolent luna moth that carries Doctor Dolittle and his companions on an adventure to the moon. Because the Doctor Dolittle series was not translated into Japanese in chronological order, the only volume of the moon trilogy that had been published in a complete Japanese translation by the time *The Luminous Fairies and Mothra* was written was the middle volume, *Doctor Dolittle in the Moon,* published in 1955 as part of the Iwanami Children's Library imprint.[60] (The prequel and sequel appeared in translation for the first time in 1961 in the twelve-volume set *The Complete Doctor Dolittle Tales* mentioned above.) There are so many elements, plot points, and images shared by the moon trilogy and *The Luminous Fairies and*

Mothra that it seems self-evident that at least one of the authors must have consulted Lofting—mostly likely in Ibuse's translation, but perhaps also in the English original or a French translation—for inspiration while brainstorming for ideas. (Nakamura, Fukunaga, and Hotta were all specialists in French literature and could read both French and English fluently.) These elements do not unfold in the same order or fashion as in Lofting's original, but the authors appear to have borrowed numerous images and plot points and rearranged them to provide the scaffolding for an entirely new story of their own making.

A brief summary should make the connections between Doctor Dolittle and Mothra clear. As Doctor Dolittle is researching the language of moths, he learns from the earthbound moths that giant moths exist on the moon, moths that, like Mothra, are "as big as a house who could lift a ton weight in the air just as though it were a feather."[61] As he learns more about moth culture, Doctor Dolittle notes that as soon as a moth hatches from its chrysalis, it seems to have an innate knowledge of the world, including not only of how to behave but also of "legends and history" that can propel them into immediate action the moment they are born. One is reminded of how Mothra's larva immediately springs into action upon hatching from the egg on Infant Island, seemingly fully aware of the creation legend and the essential role of the four fairies in the island's culture.

Not long afterward, a Mothra-sized moth appears in Doctor Dolittle's backyard. When it first appears, here's how the text describes it.

> The moth positively seemed to fill the whole garden.
>
> His shoulders behind the head, which was pressed close against the panes, towered up to a height of at least two storeys. The enormous wings were folded close to the

> thick furry body, giving the appearance of the gable end of a house—and quite as large.[62]

Despite the fact that they cannot speak the same language at first, Doctor Dolittle treats the moth with utmost respect and kindness as he nurses him back to health after the difficult journey through outer space. Eventually, Doctor Dolittle learns a rather imperfect form of communication with the giant moth, not through Earth-moth language but something more akin to telepathy, not unlike that which the fairies and Mothra share. It becomes increasingly clear to Doctor Dolittle that the moth is an extraordinarily selfless creature, and that he has made an incredibly dangerous journey to bring the animal doctor to the moon-world so that he can help the many wounded creatures living there. Before long, Doctor Dolittle and his companions are riding upon the back of the moth into space, unsure of what they will find on the moon. After arriving on the moon, the giant moth drops them off and flies away, only to reappear toward the end of *Doctor Dolittle in the Moon*.

Still, the moth is not the only commonality between the stories of Doctor Dolittle and Mothra. As the animal doctor and his companions travel over the surface of the moon, they encounter much that is reminiscent of what the characters in *The Luminous Fairies and Mothra* find on Infant Island. For instance, the moon explorers soon encounter plants that twist about and move on their own as if conscious. The overwhelming majority of the plants are benevolent, and as the doctor later learns to communicate with them, he discovers they are as complex and intelligent as human beings. However, in his conversations with the local flora, he hears that there is a one type of "vampire lily," which sends out deadly scents that ensure that "nothing round about it could exist for very long."[63] The descriptions of these plants, which are colorful, conscious, and move of their own will, suggests a direct line

Illustration by Hugh Lofting for *Doctor Dolittle in the Moon* (1928). The giant moth Jamaro Bumblelily is flying across the sky while Doctor Dolittle and his companions walk across the surface of the moon. This illustration, as well as many others, was included in Masuji Ibuse's Japanese translation published in 1955.

of influence to the "vampire plants" that attack Chūjō soon after arriving on Infant Island.

Also, early in their moon adventures, the explorers hear music wafting across the landscape, which turns out to be an unusual, rapturously beautiful form of musical communication, rather like the enticing song-speech of the Mothra fairies. The doctor soon learns it is the sentient arboreal life on the moon: "In the way that an Aeolian harp works when set in the wind at the right angle, the trees moved their branches to meet the wind. . . . It was for all the world like an orchestra. Spellbound, we stood and gazed up at them."[64] Also, around this time, the explorers discover a massive crater in the moon created by an explosion so large that they cannot at first fathom what created it. Later, Doctor Dolittle surmises that it was created by a gigantic explosion as a means to communicate via smoke signals with the giant moth while he was on Earth securing the doctor's help. Of course, Lofting wrote this book before the advent of the atomic bomb, but the description of the denuded landscape has a parallel in the nuclear desolation on Infant Island.

Like the indigenous Infant Islanders, the animal life on the moon hides for as long as possible, lingering just out of sight while warily observing the explorers. When the animal life does finally make itself visible, the animals are not diminutive creatures like the Mothra fairies. Quite the opposite—they are far larger than their terrestrial counterparts, despite being descended from them. Doctor Dolittle learns that the ecology of the moon is so stable that it produces highly nutritious food that allows everything to grow to an exceptionally large size. This is coupled with excellent governance that ensures peace and prosperity, thus letting the moon creatures reach their full potential. Although the Doctor Dolittle story emphasizes largeness and the Mothra story smallness, in both tales the authors play with physical scale, using it as an outward, visible sign of the state of civilization. In Doctor Dolittle, the creatures' large size is a sign of a prospering civilization, whereas in Mothra the small size is a sign of a smaller, vulnerable civilization that requires outside protection.

The largest and most important of the moon creatures is a seemingly immortal giant named Otho Bludge; he turns out to be the only human on the moon, cut off from other human contact for ages, much like the Infant Islanders had been cut off from surrounding civilization. Otho, it turns out, is a neolithic artist who traveled to the moon when it separated from the Earth in prehistory. At one point Otho was so lonely and desperate to draw another human that he couldn't help shouting in frustration. Out of nowhere, a beautiful fairy called Pippiteepa appears to him, sparking feelings of desire. After posing for a portrait, she disappears, crying out to him that "she could not stay—for she was of the Fairy Folk and not of his kin," and she leaves Otho alone and pining for her.[65] Although the Doctor Dolittle story has just one fairy (unlike the four in the Mothra novella or two in the film), this brief subplot may have inspired the Infant Island fairies and the novella's subplot about Chūjō developing amorous feelings for them. (When the novella was adapted for the screen, screenwriter Shin'ichi Sekizawa dispensed with Chūjō's feelings of love for the fairies, seeing it as a distraction from the main plot.)

This is not the only interesting story that Doctor Dolittle encounters. Like Fukuda on Infant Island, he learns of an ancient legend—in this case, one about the creation of the moon near the dawn of time. After the moon broke away from the Earth, human beings began to squabble with one another about religion. On one side were people who believed that the sun was the most powerful deity, but on the other were those who believed that, because the moon broke away from Earth, it was the greater of the two cosmic forces of creation. At this point, Doctor Dolittle chimes in, giving voice to Lofting's own pacifist views, saying, "The first religious strife—the first of so many. What a pity!—Just as though it mattered to any one what his neighbour believed so long as he himself led a sincere and useful life and was happy!"[66] Lofting introduces the legend not for the purpose of world-building, as in the Mothra novella, but to make a point to his readers about the folly of religious conflict. The legend that Doctor Dolittle hears does not have explicit parallels to the legend that Fukuda encounters on Infant Island, but its focus on the binary, seemingly dichotomous forces of sun and moon, of light and dark, provide yet one more point of commonality with the Mothra novella.

Eventually, after spending a good deal of time on the moon, Doctor Dolittle's assistant Stubbins gets back on board the gigantic moth and travels back to the Earth. However, when he arrives, Jamaro flies away, and Stubbins finds himself far from home. Because he has been eating so much good, nutritious food on the moon, he is now nine feet tall and towers over everyone. Without any money to get home, he joins a roadshow, which allows him to travel the countryside telling stories of his scientific discoveries and faraway adventures. He becomes a sensation on stage, and people line up to buy photographs of the now giant man, eventually providing him enough money to return home. Although these passages about the roadshow only last a few pages and are incidental to the main plot, they provide one possible source of inspiration for one of the oddest elements of the Mothra story: the decision to put the fairies, with their unusual tiny scale, on display in a public spectacle to make money.

One additional parallel between the Doctor Dolittle moon trilogy and the Mothra story has less to do with specific plot points or images and more with the general message of the stories. Although both tales are written in ways that a young reader could enjoy simply for their entertaining and quirky plots, both also contain veiled but sophisticated messages about the international order that had developed in the wake of worldwide war. In *Doctor Dolittle in the Moon*, the characters are surprised to find an almost utopian existence. One of the plants explains, "There was a day when we had constant strife, species against species, plants against plants, birds against insects, and so on. But not any more."[67] The explorers learn that Otho, the giant human, is the president of a moon-wide body called the Council that has put an end to all conflict. Otho explains:

> "At one time it was nothing but war—war, war all the time. We saw that if we did not arrange a balance we would have

> an awful mess. . . . You've seen that down there on the Earth, I imagine, have you not? . . . We just made sure, by means of the Council, that there should be *no more warfare*. . . . A new world was formed. Years after I realized that I was the one to steer and guide its destiny since I had—at that time anyway—more intelligence than the other forms of life. I saw what this fighting of kind against kind must lead to."[68]

Other passages, such as the following, go into greater detail about what the Council does.

> For example, if a certain kind of shrub wanted more room for expansion, and the territory it wished to take over was already occupied by, we'll say, bullrushes, it was not allowed to thrust out its neighbour without first submitting the case to the Council. Or if a certain kind of butterfly wished to feed upon the honey of some flower and was interfered with by a species of bee or beetle, again the argument had to be put to the vote of this all-powerful committee before any action could be taken.[69]

In these passages, Lofting seems to be describing something very much like the League of Nations, which had been founded in 1920, eight years before the publication of *Doctor Dolittle in the Moon*. This ambitious organization had been created after the end of World War I, the same war in which Lofting was wounded, to ease international tensions and prevent future wars. In its founding charter, the League of Nations set forth a goal of "promoting international co-operation" and achieving "international peace and security by the acceptance of obligations not to resort to war" and "by the prescription of open, just and honourable relations between nations."[70] In other words, Lofting appears to be using his novella to teach children how large, supranational councils like the League of Nations (or the United Nations, which was founded in 1945 right after the end of World War II) could help different populations thrive and flourish by working together within a well-established, cooperative system in which the greater good is always taken into account.

As noted above, however, Lofting's Moon Council was founded by Otho, the kind and well-intentioned giant, who serves as president. Lofting's text implies that a cooperative organization such as the League of Nations requires the strong yet benevolent guiding hand of a large power—a superpower, in other words—to organize and carry on its work. Contained in these passages is a small and implicit criticism of the fact that Lofting's adopted country, the United States, had refused to join the League of Nations due to a combination of isolationist tendencies, xenophobia, and worries about potential loss of sovereignty. If the creation of a planetwide council required a guiding superpower, then the United States in the 1920s had abandoned its moral obligations by thinking more about itself than the greater planetary good.

The Luminous Fairies and Mothra can, like *Doctor Dolittle in the Moon*, be read as a fable designed to communicate messages about the existing world order at the time of writing. Unlike the characters in the Doctor Dolittle story, who show nothing but admiration for the superpower giant Otho who leads the world order, the characters in the Mothra novella are profoundly suspicious of the superpower Rosilica, which is more concerned about adding to its own power and wealth than anything else. Superpowers do not necessarily behave with the best interests and well-being of the rest of the world in mind; they can unwittingly bring severe damage and suffering to other populations. Given this situation, it makes sense for non-superpower populations to cooperate and form their own coalitions, helping one another and protecting themselves against superpower incursions. In short, both Doctor Dolittle and Mothra present clear models of how nations ought to relate to one another, even though the two narratives come to significantly different conclusions.

Intertwining Threads of International Media

As a way of concluding this look at Mothra, I would like to point out two small details that show additional lines of connection between the Mothra story and Doctor Dolittle—this time not to highlight parallels between the written versions of the texts but to demonstrate that, even after the first iteration of each story, the mythos of the two universes continued to intertwine and influence subsequent adaptations, thus demonstrating the ways that stories can take on lives of their own as media move across national and linguistic boundaries.

As mentioned above, when the screenwriter Sekizawa adapted *The Luminous Fairies and Mothra* for the silver screen, he did away with the creation myth that appears in Fukunaga's section of the novella. Instead, he replaced it with something that might at first seem an odd substitute. Viewers of the film learn that while on Infant Island, Chūjō had discovered a rock covered with letters written in an undecipherable script that appears pictographic in nature. He deduces that this mysterious text represents a record of something important, and one of the pictographs appears to represent the symbol for Mothra—a shining sun behind a cross surrounded by lines radiating from it like the wings of a moth. Sekizawa's adaptation seems fairly random—at least until one realizes that there is an explicit parallel in *Doctor Dolittle in the Moon.* As the doctor is talking to Otho, he learns that the giant artist has been keeping a record of historical events by carving pictographs into a rock. When the doctor sees them, he finds that they "had a dash and beauty of design that would arrest the attention of almost any one."[71] In the illustration that Lofting himself has created for this scene (an illustration also reproduced in the Japanese translation published in 1955) right in the center of the rock is a pictograph featuring a large moth, and very close above it, a pictograph of a shining sun. The parallel between the rock carving in the novella and the Tōhō film is so striking that it hardly seems coincidental. As I have argued, there are far too many parallels between the moon trilogy and the Mothra novella to be mere happenstance. It seems clear the Mothra authors consulted Lofting's texts in coming up with some of the images and plot points that went into the novella, so it is entirely likely that Sekizawa, in his off-and-on consultations with the authors while working out the screenplay, would have looked at Lofting's book too. After all, several chapters featured a gigantic moth, very much of the type that Sekizawa was working to put on screen. In short, even after the publication of the novella, Lofting's book appears to have exerted a silent and unacknowledged influence on the unfolding Mothra universe.

In 1962, Columbia Pictures released a slightly abridged, dubbed version of *Mothra* to movie theaters in the English-speaking world where it made a healthy profit thanks to its colorful imagery, quirky story, and charming monster. One critic, reviewing it for the *New York Times,* praised the "color, as pretty as can be, that now and then smites the eye with some genuinely artistic panoramas and décor designs" as well as the "genuinely penetrating moments, such as the contrast of the approaching terror and those patient, silvery-voiced little 'dolls,' serenely awaiting rescue." The same critic also called some of special-effect shots "brilliant," although he panned the "clumsy and absurd" dialogue and the ham-fisted comic relief of actor Frankie Sakai in the role of Fukuda.[72] It seems clear that Columbia didn't anticipate that American audiences would take the story as seriously as Nakamura, Fukunaga, and Hotta had hoped, considering that when they sent out *Mothra* to theaters, it was usually as a B-film—in other words, the secondary, lesser film in a double

Illustration by Hugh Lofting for *Doctor Dolittle in the Moon* (1928). The pictographs depicted here resemble the rock-carved symbols that appear in the 1961 film *Mothra,* suggesting a line of influence not just from the Doctor Dolittle books to the novella but to the film adaptation as well.

---

feature. For instance, in July 1962 in Los Angeles, *Mothra* appeared in twenty-four theaters coupled with a now largely forgotten comedy called *Zotz!* that the *Los Angeles Times* described as "nonsense in helter-skelter style."[73] That same month in New York, *Mothra* played alongside the newly released slapstick film *The Three Stooges in Orbit.* The following year, Columbia Pictures was still shopping it around as part of a double feature, this time alongside its new 1963 youth-oriented adventure film *Jason and the Argonauts.*[74]

There is a hint that as the film *Mothra* traveled through the English-speaking world, it did attract the notice of people interested in Doctor Dolittle. Toward the end of the film is a scene that has no parallel in the novella. While Mothra is attacking New Kirk City and causing massive chaos, Chūjō and his companions think of a way to get Mothra to settle down so they can bring about a reunion with the kidnapped fairies. Chūjō asks the authorities to paint a gigantic version of the symbol he discovered in the rock carving, the same symbol that he believes to mean "Mothra." When the authorities do so, Mothra calms down. Treating the symbol like the airplane guides on an airport tarmac, the gigantic moth lands, and the moth and fairies reunite. Moments later, the fairies ride off on Mothra's back toward Infant Island, and the film ends.

In late 1967, five years after the international release of *Mothra,* Twentieth Century–Fox released the big-budget musical film *Doctor Dolittle,* directed by Richard Fleischer and starring Rex Harrison in the title role. The film is a rather free rearrangement of plotlines culled from various parts of the Lofting series with a handful of other new elements, such as a love interest for the doctor, thrown in to generate interest on screen. One of the newly added elements comes in the last scene of the film, which is so strikingly similar to the last scenes of the film *Mothra* that the line of influence is difficult to deny. At this point, Doctor Dolittle is stranded on a floating island in the ocean. After deciding to return to England, the doctor calls upon a giant luna moth to carry him there. His method of beckoning the moth involves drawing a gigantic symbol of a moth on the ground and asking the indigenous inhabitants of the island to sit upon it, thus drawing the moth's attention with the shape. Sure enough, just as in the film *Mothra,* the gigantic moth-like symbol on the ground does the trick; a giant luna moth appears, and the film ends with scenes of the doctor flying through a moonlit sky back to Britain.[75]

The undeniable similarities between the ending of the film *Mothra* and the film *Doctor Dolittle* are evidence of transnational circulation within the entertainment industry, as images travel across genres, languages, and national boundaries. In this final scene, we see the completion of a loop of influences, which starts with the Doctor Dolittle series of books inspiring scenes in the Mothra novella, and then the Mothra film inspiring scenes in the Doctor Dolittle film. In this chain of interlocking influences we also see the completion of an almost perfect geographical loop, which starts with a story by a British writer living in America being translated into Japanese; that story then inspires a novella that is turned into a Japanese film, one that subsequently travels to America and influences aspects of an American film starring a British actor.

When considered as a pair, there is something poetic about how these two films end. In the final scene of the 1961 *Mothra,* the main characters are in a large country seeing off the gigantic moth, watching it retreat into the distance toward a small island in the ocean. In the 1967 film *Doctor Dolittle* the gaze is reversed, with the inhabitants of a small island seeing off the gigantic moth as it travels to a large nation. This trajectory shows us that even on opposite sides of the world, no one is entirely alone. There are people standing on one shore, looking out, admiring and absorbing what they see in the distance, whereas on the opposite shore, others are looking back, doing exactly the same thing.

Notes

1. Although Kayama's enormous contribution to the 1954 film *Godzilla* is well known in Japan, his name has barely appeared in any of the English-language discussions of the history of the film, despite the fact that his name appears in large letters on screen as the second credit in the film itself. For a corrective to this oversight, see Kayama, *Godzilla and Godzilla Raids Again.*

2. There are numerous sources about the history of the 1954 film *Godzilla.* The most careful and thorough one in Japanese is the recently published Gurūpu Kenkyū Kyokuhon, *1954 Gojira: Kenkyū kyokuhon.* In English, helpful sources include Kalat, *A Critical History and Filmography of Toho's Godzilla® Series;* Ryfle and Godziszewski, *Ishirō Honda,* 83–107; and Angles, "Afterword: Translating an Icon," 189–207. Of course, there are countless analyses of the cultural significance and underlying meanings of *Godzilla.* In English, important recent studies include Igarashi, *Bodies of Memory,* 114–21; Tsutsui, *Godzilla® on My Mind;* Tsutsui and Ito, *In Godzilla's® Footsteps;* Barr, *The Kaiju Film;* Rhoads and McCorkle, "Chapter 3: *Godzilla,* Nature and Nuclear Revenge."
3. Skipper, *Godzilla,* 30.
4. Ryfle and Godziszewski, *Ishirō Honda,* 191.
5. Nakamura, "Atogaki: Kaisō '*Mosura,*'" 170.
6. Cited in Ryfle and Godziszewski, *Ishirō Honda,* 173.
7. Keene, *Dawn to the West,* 2:1006–7.
8. Nakamura, "Atogaki," 170.
9. There are enough of these collaboratively produced mystery novels from the early to mid-twentieth century that one publisher of popular fiction has recently produced an eight-volume set of them: Kusaka, *Gassaku tantei shōsetsu.* One should note that a significant number of these collaborative projects were abandoned in mid-serialization. Although the collaborative format could produce entertaining plot twists, it also sometimes produced problems, especially when authors had a short deadline. If a receiving author had trouble figuring out what to do next with the story, they might not submit a manuscript on time.
10. Keene, *Dawn to the West,* 2:1008.
11. Keene, 2:1008.
12. This novel has been translated as Fukunaga, *Flowers of Grass.*
13. Bourdaghs, "Monstrous Melodies and Island Fantasies," 11–12.
14. Nakamura, "Atogaki," 170.
15. In translating this text, I've relied on two reprints: Nakamura, Fukunaga, and Hotta, *Hakkō yōsei to Mosura,* 1994, 3–82; and Nakamura, Fukunaga, and Hotta, *"Hakkō yōsei to Mosura,"* 1998, 62–107.
16. Specifically, *The Luminous Fairies and Mothra* does not appear in any of the following collections: Nakamura, *Nakamura Shin'ichirō shōsetsu shūsei;* Fukunaga, *Fukunaga Takehiko zenshū;* Hotta, *Hotta Yoshie zenshū,* 1974; Hotta, *Hotta Yoshie zenshū,* 1993. Although I've suggested above that copyrights might have been one reason for this, perhaps another lies with the fact that each of these sets brings together only the work of one of the three authors. It is easy to imagine that the editors of

these collections of "complete" or "collected" works didn't feel that the novella, which was written by three people, fit well with the individual authors' other single-authored works.

17. Welfield, *An Empire in Eclipse,* 25.
18. Cited in Jesty, "Tokyo 1960."
19. Jesty.
20. Jesty.
21. Jesty.
22. Kapur, *Japan at the Crossroads,* 13.
23. Kapur, 29.
24. Kapur, 33.
25. Kapur, 34.
26. Ryfle and Godziszewski, *Ishirō Honda,* 176.
27. Ryfle and Godziszewski, 178.
28. Ono, *Mosura no seishinshi,* 63.
29. In Japanese, three useful comparisons of the novella and film can be found in Ono, *Mosura no seishinshi;* Hosokawa, "Tōhō tokusatsu eiga '*Mosura*' to Nakamura Shin'ichirō, Fukunaga Takehiko, Hotta Yoshie no '*Hakkō yōsei to Mosura*'"; and Yoshitani, "Nakamura Shin'ichirō, Fukunaga Takehiko, Hotta Yoshie '*Hakkō yōsei to Mosura*' ni okeru Hotta Yoshie pāto."
30. Nakamura, "Atogaki," 171–72.
31. Watanabe, *The Architecture of Tôkyô,* 117.
32. Ono, 64–65.
33. See the interesting discussion about the difference in nuance between the two words at Michiura, "Shin kotoba jijō *9485.*"
34. Yoshitani, "Nakamura Shin'ichirō, Fukunaga Takehiko, Hotta Yoshie '*Hakkō yōsei to Mosura*' ni okeru Hotta Yoshie pāto," 20. The passage where the word substitution has taken place appears right before the section about the Infant Islanders' creation myth: Nakamura, Fukunaga, and Hotta, *Hakkō yōsei to Mosura,* 1994, 26.
35. One exception was the Marshall Islands, located in the eastern part of Micronesia. This island chain was so distant that few Japanese settled there, finding it too isolated to be economically profitable. (The Marshall Islands, one should remember, was the remote island chain where, later in the 1950s, the U.S. military conducted its hydrogen bomb tests.) Peattie, "Chapter 4: The Nan'yō," 197.
36. History.com, "Tony-winning Musical 'South Pacific' Opens on Broadway | April 7, 1949."

37. Yaguchi, *Akogare no Hawai.* On the fascination for hula in Japan, see Ogiwara, "Gendai Nihon ni okeru Hawai no dentō buyō hura no ichizuke."
38. "D-Day for Japanese Tourist."
39. Ryfle and Godziszewski, 176.
40. Bourdaghs.
41. Ono, 80–81.
42. Cited in Ono, 74.
43. Kirsten, *The Book of Tiki,* 42.
44. For a famous discussion of mimicry, see Bhabha, "Chapter 4: Of Mimicry and Man."
45. Igarashi, "Mothra's Gigantic Egg," 88.
46. Tierney, *Tropics of Savagery,* 4–5.
47. When asked in interviews about the use of the name "Infant Island," the film screenwriter Shin'ichi Sekizawa tended to give vague answers, such as "because it was a cheerful place," or "the name Infant Island didn't have any meaning at all," but it seems doubtful that Sekizawa was the one who came up with the name in the first place. Ono, *Mosura no seishinshi,* 74.
48. Nakamura, "Atogaki," 171.
49. Ono, 30–33.
50. Nakamura, "Atogaki," 171.
51. Barr, *The Kaiju Film,* 94.
52. Interestingly, when I translated Shigeru Kayama's 1955 novellas *Godzilla and Godzilla Raids Again* for publication a few years ago, I found that these early texts by the author who wrote the screenplays to the 1954 and 1955 films made no reference whatsoever to Godzilla's gender. (See my comments on this in Angles, "Translator's Afterword," 218–19.) It was in later subtitles and popular commentary that Godzilla came to be gendered as specifically male. Tōhō Studios' official stance, at least in recent decades, is that Godzilla does not have a specific gender and should be described using the gender-neutral pronoun "it"—a trend that one sees in the studio's subtitles for the 2023 blockbuster *Godzilla Minus One.*
53. Although this is speculation, it is not impossible that this was a mistake in the original. One could imagine that perhaps an earlier draft of the story had used the masculine pronoun, but at some point, a decision was made to change this, and all instances were eliminated except for in this one spot, which was accidentally left unchecked before sending the manuscript to the typesetter. In the age before word processors and computers, Japanese authors typically wrote by hand on a special

type of manuscript paper. Editors would then write their changes directly in the manuscript before submitting it to the typesetter. Since all instances of *kare* appear within close proximity to one another, it is perhaps possible that an editor missed this page, or perhaps an old version of that particular page somehow slipped in where an edited page should have been. Without the original handwritten manuscript, it is impossible to confirm this possibility.

54. Lofting, *Complete Works,* "Doctor Dolittle's Garden," Part 2, Chap. 9.
55. For more on Lofting's experiences with war and his subsequent pacifism, see Williams, "Hugh Lofting (1886–1947)."
56. Cited in Blishen, "Hugh Lofting," 16. Although Lofting was a progressive voice for his time, not all of his work completely lived up to his own ideals. In particular, the language used to describe Africans and South American Indians reflect the stereotypes and prejudicial language that circulated at the time and have not weathered well. His uncomfortable depictions have caused consternation and condemnation among contemporary readers, much like the depictions of the Japanese actors wearing blackface in *Mothra* cause discomfort today. For this reason, Hugh Lofting's son Christopher has permitted these sections to be modified in new editions of Lofting's work. On these textual changes, see Williams, "Hugh Lofting (1886–1947)," 39.
57. Ozaki, *Himitsu no ōkoku,* 216.
58. Cited in Ozaki, 241.
59. One of my friends who grew up in the immediate postwar period mentioned to me that she looked forward to the publication of the new Doctor Dolittle books with the same frenzied passion that English readers around the turn of the twenty-first century looked forward to the publication of new installments of J. K. Rowling's Harry Potter series.
60. Lofting, *Doritoru sensei tsuki e yuku.*
61. Lofting, *Complete Works,* "Doctor Dolittle's Garden," Part 2, Chap. 10.
62. Lofting, *Complete Works,* "Doctor Dolittle's Garden," Part 3, Chap. 3.
63. Lofting, *Complete Works,* "Doctor Dolittle in the Moon," Chap. 14.
64. Lofting, *Complete Works,* "Doctor Dolittle in the Moon," Chap. 8.
65. Lofting, *Complete Works,* "Doctor Dolittle in the Moon," Chap. 16.
66. Lofting, *Complete Works,* "Doctor Dolittle in the Moon," Chap. 16.
67. Lofting, *Complete Works,* "Doctor Dolittle in the Moon," Chap. 17.
68. Lofting, *Complete Works,* "Doctor Dolittle in the Moon," Chap. 21. Emphasis in original.
69. Lofting, *Complete Works,* "Doctor Dolittle in the Moon," Chap. 18.
70. United Nations Office at Geneva, "The Covenant of the League of Nations."

71. Lofting, *Complete Works,* "Doctor Dolittle in the Moon," Chap. 23.
72. Weiler, "Screen."
73. Harford, "'Zotz!' Film Fantasy Heavy on Slapstick."
74. See "Neighborhood Movie Attractions"; "Sidney Lust Theatres [Classified Ad]."
75. Fleischer (dir.), *Doctor Dolittle,* 2:20:00.

Bibliography

Angles, Jeffrey. "Afterword: Translating an Icon." In *Godzilla and Godzilla Raids Again,* by Shigeru Kayama, 189–221. Minneapolis: University of Minnesota Press, 2023.

Barr, Jason. *The Kaiju Film: A Critical Study of Cinema's Biggest Monsters.* Jefferson, N.C.: McFarland & Co., 2016.

Bhabha, Homi K. "Chapter 4. Of Mimicry and Man: The Ambivalence of Colonial Discourse." In *The Location of Culture,* reprint, 121–32. Routledge Classics. New York: Routledge, 2004.

Blishen, Edward. "Hugh Lofting." In *The Bodley Head Monographs.* London: Bodley Head, 1968.

Bourdaghs, Michael. "Monstrous Melodies and Island Fantasies: Mothra, The Peanuts, and Japan's Cold War Cultures." *The Asia-Pacific Journal: Japan Focus* 22, no. 4 (April 30, 2024). https://apjjf.org/wp-content/uploads/2024/04/Article_5840.pdf.

Edogawa Ranpo, Yokomizo Seishi, Kōga Saburō, Ōshita Udaru, Yumeno Kyūsaku, and Morishita Uson. *Egawa Ranko.* Tokyo: Shun'yōdō Shoten, 1993.

Fleischer, Richard (director). *Doctor Dolittle.* Streaming video. 20th Century Fox, 1967. https://www.amazon.com/Doctor-Dolittle-Rex-Harrison/dp/B000I9X7CQ.

Fukunaga, Takehiko. *Flowers of Grass.* Translated by Royall Tyler. Champaign, Ill.: Dalkey Archive Press, 2012.

Fukunaga Takehiko. *Fukunaga Takehiko zenshū.* 20 vols. Tokyo: Shinchōsha, 1986.

Fukunaga Takehiko. *Kusa no hana.* Tokyo: Shinchōsha, 1956.

Gurūpu Kenkyū Kyokuhon, ed. *1954 Gojira: Kenkyū kyokuhon.* Tokyo: Hobby Japan, 2024.

Harford, Margaret. "'Zotz!' Film Fantasy Heavy on Slapstick." *Los Angeles Times,* June 29, 1962, C10.

History.com. "Tony-winning Musical 'South Pacific' Opens on Broadway

| April 7, 1949." History, April 4, 2024. https://www.history.com/this-day-in-history/south-pacific-musical-opens-broadway-1949.
Honda, Ishirō (director). *Godzilla.* Criterion Channel. Streaming video. Tōhō, 1954. https://www.criterionchannel.com/videos/godzilla.
Honda, Ishirō (director). *King Kong vs. Godzilla.* DVD. Universal Pictures, 1962.
Honda Ishirō (director). *Mosura.* Toho DVD Masterpiece Selection. DVD. Tōhō, 1961.
Honda, Ishirō (director). *Radon.* Amazon Prime. Streaming Video. Tōhō, 1956. https://amzn.to/4jMHiZV.
Honda, Ishirō (director). *The Mysterians.* Criterion Channel. Streaming Video. Tōhō, 1957. https://www.criterionchannel.com/videos/the-mysterians.
Honda, Ishirō (director). *Varan the Unbelievable.* Criterion Channel. Streaming Video. Tōhō, 1958. https://www.criterionchannel.com/videos/varan-the-unbelievable.
Hosokawa Ryōichi. "Tōhō tokusatsu eiga *'Mosura'* to Nakamura Shin'ichirō, Fukunaga Takehiko, Hotta Yoshie no *'Hakkō yōsei to Mosura.'*" *Kyōto Tachibana Daigaku kenkyū kiyō* 41 (2015): 19–31.
Hotta Yoshie. *Hiroba no kodoku.* Tokyo: Shinchōsha, 1953.
Hotta Yoshie. *Hotta Yoshie zenshū.* 16 vols. Tokyo: Chikuma Shobō, 1974.
Hotta Yoshie. *Hotta Yoshie zenshū.* 16 vols. Tokyo: Chikuma Shobō, 1993.
Hotta Yoshie. *Indo de kangaeta koto.* Tokyo: Iwanami Shinsho, 1957.
Ibuse, Masuji. *Black Rain.* Translated by John Bester. New York: Kodansha International, 2012.
Ibuse, Masuji. "The Crazy Iris." In *The Crazy Iris and Other Stories of the Atomic Aftermath,* edited by Kenzaburō Ōe, translated by Ivan Morris, 17–37. New York: Grove Press, 1985.
Ibuse Masuji. *Yōhai taichō, Honjitsu kyūshin.* Tokyo: Shinchō Bunko, 2014.
Igarashi, Yoshikuni. *Bodies of Memory: Narratives of War in Postwar Japanese Culture, 1945–1970.* Princeton, N.J.: Princeton University Press, 2000.
Igarashi, Yoshikuni. "Mothra's Gigantic Egg: Consuming the South Pacific in 1960s Japan." In *In Godzilla's® Footsteps: Japanese Pop Culture Icons on the Global Stage,* edited by William Tsutsui and Michiko Ito, 83–102. New York: Palgrave Macmillan, 2006.
Inagaki, Hiroshi (director). *The Three Treasures.* Internet Archive. Streaming Video. Tōhō, 1959. https://archive.org/details/l35300610.
Jesty, Justin. "Tokyo 1960: Days of Rage & Grief: Hamaya Hiroshi's Photos of the Anti-Security-Treaty Protests." MIT Visualizing Cultures, 2012. https://visualizingcultures.mit.edu/tokyo_1960/anp2_essay01.html.
Kalat, David. *A Critical History and Filmography of Toho's Godzilla® Series.* 2nd ed. Jefferson, N.C.: McFarland & Co., 2017.

Kapur, Nick. *Japan at the Crossroads: Conflict and Compromise after Anpo.* Cambridge, Mass.: Harvard University Press, 2018.

Kayama, Shigeru. *Godzilla and Godzilla Raids Again.* Translated by Jeffrey Angles. Minneapolis: University of Minnesota Press, 2023.

Keene, Donald. *Dawn to the West: Japanese Literature in the Modern Era, Fiction.* Vol. 2. New York: Columbia University Press, 1998.

Kirsten, Sven A. *The Book of Tiki: The Cult of Polynesia Pop in Fifties America.* Cologne: Taschen, 2000.

Kusaka Sanzō, ed. *Gassaku tantei shōsetsu.* 8 vols. Tokyo: Shun'yōdō, 2022.

Lofting, Hugh. *Complete Works.* Delphi Classics 11. Kindle. Hastings, East Sussex: Delphi Classics, 2020.

Lofting, Hugh. *Doritoru sensei tsuki e yuku.* Translated by Ibuse Masuji. Iwanami Shōnen Bunko 107. Tokyo: Iwanami Shoten, 1955.

Michener, James A. *Minami taiheiyō monogatari.* Translated by Shimizu Shunji. Tokyo: Rokkō Shuppansha, 1952.

Michener, James A. *Tales of the South Pacific.* New York: Dial Press, 2014.

Michiura Toshihiko. "Shin kotoba jijō 9485: 'Senjūmin ka? Genjūmin ka?'" *Michiura Toshihiko TIME | Yomiuri Terebi,* July 11, 2024. https://www.ytv.co.jp/michiura_time/contents/202407/5t9qscgbkuk8id87.html.

Nakamura Shin'ichirō. "Atogaki: Kaisō '*Mosura.*'" In *Hakkō yōsei to Mosura,* by Nakamura Shin'ichirō, Fukunaga Takehiko, and Hotta Yoshie, 169–72. Tokyo: Chikuma Shobō, 1994.

Nakamura Shin'ichirō. *Kaiten mokuba.* Reprint. Tokyo: Kōdansha, 1975.

Nakamura Shin'ichirō. *Kokū no bara.* Tokyo: Kōdansha, 1957.

Nakamura Shin'ichirō. *Nakamura Shin'ichirō shōsetsu shūsei.* 13 vols. Tokyo: Shinchōsha, 1992.

Nakamura Shin'ichirō. *Shi no kage no shita ni.* Vol. 2. *Nakamura Shin'ichirō shōsetsu shūsei.* Tokyo, 1992.

Nakamura Shin'ichirō, Fukunaga Takehiko, and Hotta Yoshie. *Hakkō yōsei to Mosura.* Tokyo: Chikuma Shobō, 1994.

Nakamura Shin'ichirō, Fukunaga Takehiko, and Hotta Yoshie. "*Hakkō yōsei to Mosura.*" In *Kaijū bungaku taizen,* edited by Higashi Masao, 62–107. Tokyo: Kawade Bunko, 1998.

"Neighborhood Movie Attractions." *Washington Post and Times Herald,* September 29, 1963, G2.

New York Times. "D-Day for Japanese Tourist—Ban on Pleasure Trips Abroad Will Be Lifted April 1—Many Expected to Visit Hawaii and U.S. Mainland." February 9, 1964.

Oda, Motoyoshi (director). *Godzilla Raids Again.* Criterion Channel. Streaming video. Tōhō, 1955. https://www.criterionchannel.com/videos/godzilla-raids-again.

Ogiwara Tomomi. "Gendai Nihon ni okeru Hawai no dentō buyō hura no ichizuke: Yobiteki kōsatsu." *Ongaku kenkyū: Daigakuin kenkyū nenpō* 33 (March 2021): 217–32.

Ono Shuntarō. *Mosura no seishinshi.* Kōdansha gendai shinsho 1901. Tokyo: Kōdansha, 2007.

Ozaki Mariko. *Himitsu no ōkoku: Hyōden Ishii Momoko.* Tokyo: Shinchōsha, 2014.

Peattie, Mark R. "Chapter 4: The Nan'yō: Japan in the South Pacific, 1885–1945." In *The Japanese Colonial Empire, 1895–1945,* edited by Ramon H. Myers and Mark R. Peattie, 172–210. Princeton, N.J.: Princeton University Press, 2020.

Rhoads, Sean, and Brooke McCorkle. "Chapter 3: *Godzilla,* Nature and Nuclear Revenge." In *Japan's Green Monsters: Environmental Commentary in Kaiju Cinema,* 34–49. Jefferson, N.C.: McFarland & Co., 2018.

Ryfle, Steve, and Ed Godziszewski. *Ishirō Honda: A Life in Film, from Godzilla to Kurosawa.* Middletown, Conn.: Wesleyan University Press, 2017.

"Sidney Lust Theatres [Classified Ad]." *Washington Post and Times Herald,* October 2, 1963, C9.

Skipper, Graham. *Godzilla: The Official Guide to the King of the Monsters.* London: Welbeck, 2022.

Tierney, Robert Thomas. *Tropics of Savagery: The Culture of Japanese Empire in Comparative Frame.* Asia Pacific Modern 5. Berkeley: University of California Press, 2010.

Tsutsui, William. *Godzilla® on My Mind: Fifty Years of the King of Monsters.* New York: Palgrave Macmillan, 2004.

Tsutsui, William, and Michiko Ito, eds. *In Godzilla's® Footsteps: Japanese Pop Culture Icons on the Global Stage.* New York: Palgrave Macmillan, 2006.

United Nations Office at Geneva. "The Covenant of the League of Nations." Accessed February 4, 2025. https://www.ungeneva.org/en/about/league-of-nations/covenant.

Watanabe, Hiroshi. *The Architecture of Tôkyô: An Architectural History in 571 Individual Presentations.* Stuttgart: Edition Axel Menges, 2001.

Weiler, A. H. "Screen: 'Hatari!' Captures the Drama of Tanganyika Wildlife: Howard Hawks Film Opens at DeMille Neighborhood Houses Offer 2 Twin Bills." *New York Times,* July 12, 1962. https://web.archive.org/web/20200707202041/https%3A%2F%2Fwww.nytimes.com%2F1962%2F07%2F12%2Farchives%2Fscreen-hatari-captures-the-drama-of-tanganyika-wildlifehoward-hawks.html.

Welfield, John. *An Empire in Eclipse: Japan in the Postwar American Alliance System.* Bloomsbury Academic Collections: Japanese Politics and International Relations. London: Bloomsbury, 2013.

Williams, Kathleen Broome. "Hugh Lofting (1886–1947)." In *From Soldier to Storyteller: Essays on World War Veterans Who Became Famous Children's Authors,* edited by Williams and Hal M. Friedman, 33–48. Jefferson, N.C.: McFarland & Co., 2024.

Yaguchi Yūjin. *Akogare no Hawai: Nihonjin no Hawai-kan.* Tokyo: Chūō Kōron Shinsha, 2011.

Yoshitani Hiroya. "Nakamura Shin'ichirō, Fukunaga Takehiko, Hotta Yoshie *'Hakkō yōsei to Mosura'* ni okeru Hotta Yoshie pāto." *Gunpō* 9 (March 2024): 19–36.

Shin'ichirō Nakamura 中村真一郎 (1918–1997) was a novelist, critic, and scholar known for his literary and philosophical writings after World War II. His novel *Under the Shadow of Death* explores the experiences of intellectuals living through militarism and fascism. He was an esteemed translator of French literature and a literary historian who wrote about Japanese classics.

Takehiko Fukunaga 福永武彦 (1918–1979) was a prolific novelist and poet recognized for his introspective, often melancholic style. His novel *Flowers of Grass,* about a bisexual young man exploring love and art while sick with tuberculosis, is a classic of Japanese postwar literature. Deeply influenced by French literature and existentialism, he translated works by many French writers, including Baudelaire, Gide, and Greene. He also wrote crime fiction under the pen name Reitarō Kada and science fiction under the pen name Gaku Funada.

Yoshie Hotta 堀田善衛 (1918–1998) was a novelist and essayist known for his historical and politically engaged fiction. His writing often examined cultural identity in the modern world and the contributions of writers and intellectuals to shifts in the course of history. He wrote extensively on world history and politics, reflecting his international perspective. He was a strong advocate for peace and democracy, and his literature is an important representation of Japan's modern history.

Jeffrey Angles is a professor of Japanese literature at Western Michigan University and an award-winning translator of Japanese literature. He is the author of *Writing the Love of Boys* (Minnesota, 2011), and his translations include the modernist classic *The Book of the Dead* by Shinobu Orikuchi (Minnesota, 2016) and *Godzilla and Godzilla Raids Again* by Shigeru Kayama (Minnesota, 2023).